Resisting THE BIKER

Cassie Alexandra

Copyright ©2015 by Cassie Alexandra/K.L. Middleton

All rights reserved.

No part of this book may be reproduced, or stored in a retrieval system or transmitted in any form or by any means, electronic, mechanical, photocopying, recording, or otherwise without express written permission of the author.

This book is purely fiction. Any resemblances to names, characters, and places are coincidental. The reproduction of this work is forbidden without written consent from the author.

Prologue

It was just after nine o'clock p.m. when Jessica Winters walked out of *Twenty-Four Hour Fitness*, dropped her gym bag into the trunk of her car, and drove to her two-bedroom apartment in Iowa City. She pulled into the underground garage, grabbed her things, and headed toward the elevator, relieved that her roommate, Kellie, was out of town. She'd have the place to herself for a couple of days, which meant that she wouldn't have to listen to the sound of Kellie and her boyfriend, Jack, going at it in the other room all hours of the night. She had to admit, listening to Kellie when she was having those 'mind-blowing orgasms', as she so fondly called them, was hell. Especially for someone who'd decided not to have sex until she met the 'one'. 'The *one*' who seemed to be taking his damn sweet time in finding her.

"You should get yourself a vibrator," said Kellie after Jessica had confronted her about keeping the noise down the previous weekend. "Maybe you wouldn't be so weird about it."

"If not wanting to listen to other people having sex is being weird then I certainly don't want to be whatever it is you consider normal."

"God, you take everything so fucking seriously. I'm just giving you shit. Although," she'd smirked, "you have to admit, you're way too uptight about sex. You're twenty years old, for God's sake. You need to get your freak on, Jessica, like the rest of us."

"I'm not uptight and I don't need to 'get my freak on'. I'm just tired from not getting any sleep," she'd shot back angrily. "I mean, come on – *four* in the morning? You'd be pissed, too, if you had classes at seven and were up all night, trying to block out the howling in the next room. If you could at least keep it down. That's all I ask."

"Honey, you can't keep good sex down. If you had it, you'd know what I mean."

"Whatever. At least turn up the damn music."

"Fine."

The truth was that they fought about more than just the obnoxious grunting and moaning coming from Kellie's room. They argued about groceries, cable and electric bills, or where things belonged in the apartment. It certainly wasn't fun going home at night, and Jessica pretty much knew what she had to do – find herself a new roommate or… move back in with her mother, Frannie. At least she'd get more sleep and not have to put up with Kellie's bullshit. Unfortunately, that meant she'd also have to move in with Slammer, her mom's biker fiancé. Not only was he intimidating, but he was the president of the Gold Vipers, a motorcycle club in Jensen, which Jessica wanted absolutely no part of. Admittedly, she actually liked Slammer and he was not at all what she'd expected, with his easy-going manner and funny stories. Sure, every other word was 'fuck' and he smoked like a chimney, but he treated Frannie, his 'Old Lady" as he liked to call her, like a queen *and* he was even considerate to Jessica. But, as far as she was concerned, he was still in a gang and his way of living wasn't the kind she wanted for her mother. She'd even tried talking Frannie out of seeing Slammer several times, but apparently the two of them had already fallen "hopelessly in love", so it was like talking to a wall. Even when Jessica mentioned the fact that bikers in clubs like his were always breaking the law and ending up in prison, she'd come back with – "Slammer says that the Gold Vipers aren't like other MC clubs. They're more like a band of brothers who look out for each other and their families. Everything they are involved with is totally legit."

Yeah, right.

Frannie was so gullible, it was frustrating. Jessica could only cross her fingers and hope that Slammer would keep her out of anything illegal. If he did try to involve her mother in any way, and she got word of it, Slammer would find his ass in jail faster than he could light his next Camel. Her mother meant everything to her and there was no way she'd sit back quietly or turn the other cheek. Frannie was close to retirement and she didn't want her mother spending any part of it in prison.

Looking forward to a quiet night, Jessica pushed the thoughts of her future stepdad away, and took the elevator to the third floor. Humming to herself, she walked down the hallway to her apartment, unlocked the door, and slipped inside. As she was about to turn the kitchen light on, someone grabbed her from behind, his arm locking around her like a steel vice. She tried to scream but it was immediately cut off by a gloved hand clamping over her mouth. The smell of leather and gasoline made her gag.

"Hello, darlin'," the man growled into her. He began groping her breasts. "Oh, these are nice."

Sobbing, she tried struggling, but it only made him laugh. Desperate to get away, she tried biting his hand through the glove.

"Bitch," he snarled, squeezing her mouth so hard, her jaw ached. "Fight me and you die. Understand?"

Whimpering, Jessica ignored his threat and slammed her elbow into his stomach, remembering the self-defense class she'd taken before college. The instructor had said to fight for your life at any cost. Scream, kick, do whatever it took to get away, or the chances of surviving were slim to none.

The man grunted, but instead of releasing her, he grabbed her by the throat and began to squeeze. "You think you have a chance against me, bitch? You keep fighting, and I'll snap your neck. Don't you dare fucking test me!"

"Please... can't... breathe..." she begged hoarsely.

He loosened his hold slightly. "You gonna behave?"

Her mind was whirling as she tried to think of another way of escape. The kitchen knives were too far out of reach and he was so strong. She'd never make it.

"Answer me, bitch!" he hissed, pulling her hair back cruelly in his fist.

"Yes!" she cried.

"Okay then," he whispered, pushing her toward the bedroom. "Now, let's go have us some fun."

***

An hour later, Jessica heard him leave the apartment. Bloody and bruised, she staggered back to the kitchen, locking the door. Then, she grabbed her cell phone and called nine-one-one.

"I've been attacked. Raped," she sobbed into the phone, her entire body shaking. She slid down to the floor, glancing at the doorway in terror, worried he'd bust it down and kill her. "Please... help me. I'm afraid he'll come back."

"We're sending someone right away," the woman promised, trying to calm her down. "You are sure that the assailant has left?"

"Yes," she replied, staring down at the bruises on her thighs where he'd dug his fingers into her flesh. Between that and the burning pain between her legs, she wanted to die. She wanted *him* to die.

"Okay. The police should be there soon," reminded the operator. "I'll stay on the phone with you until they arrive. Did you get a good look at the assailant?"

"He... he wore a mask. A black one."

"Did you recognize his voice?"

"No. Nobody I know would do this!"

"Okay. Try to calm down, Ms. Winters. Someone is coming."

As Jessica waited for help to arrive, she closed her eyes and began crying all over again. The woman on the phone tried soothing her, but all she could think about was the rapist's gloating brown eyes. She'd never forget them or his dry, cracked lips. He'd made her stare up at him while he did the unspeakable. It seemed to get him off.

"You see me?" he'd growled several times.

Jessica had seen him clearly. He was the devil. He even wore a patch on his vest that proved it.

Chapter One

Jensen, Iowa

Adriana

"You ready for this?" asked Krystal, turning off the engine of her '76 Monte Carlo. We'd just pulled into the parking lot of Griffin's, a strip club on the edge of town. It was her twenty-first birthday and her boyfriend, the owner's son, had asked us to meet him before we hooked up with the rest of our friends downtown.

I looked at the seedy dive, with its flashing lights and line of shiny motorcycles parked on the side. I'd never been inside, but everyone knew the place was bad news. I couldn't even imagine the look on my mother's face if she knew I was even considering going inside. She'd probably think I'd starting smoking crack.

I shivered. "Seriously? Can't we just meet him out here, in the parking lot?"

"What's wrong?" she asked, pulling down the visor. She fluffed out her blond hair and then reached down to adjust her push-up bra, emphasizing the curve of her boobs in the sparkly, black tank she'd managed to cram them into. "You nervous about walking into a biker bar?"

"It's more than that and you know it." The place had a bad reputation – gangs, brawls, drug deals, and prostitution.

"Chill out, girl. Nothing is going to happen inside. You're with me and everyone knows that *I'm* with the owner's son."

I sighed. "Okay."

"You're good?"

"Yes. I'm good."

Krystal smirked. "Liar. Here, take a shot of this," she said, pulling out a bottle of peach-flavored schnapps from under the seat. "It'll take the edge off."

"Schnapps?"

She uncapped the bottle and took a long pull. "Mm… yeah. Here." She held it out.

"Maybe we should wait until we leave the club."

"No, babe. We need to get this party rolling."

"Fine," I replied, taking the bottle from her. I took a swig and my stomach immediately felt warm and tingly. "Hmm… Not bad. A little sweet but I like it."

"I'm surprised you've never tried it."

"Actually, I think I did. I had one of those drinks, Sex On The Beach, when we went out for my twenty-first. I think this was in it."

She took another swig. "I love those and Fuzzy Navels. You've got to try one. Those are fucking excellent."

I wasn't sure what a Fuzzy Navel was, but if it involved the peach-flavored schnapps, I was definitely in.

"Okay," she said, capping the bottle. "Let's go see what the hell Tank wants."

Tank, her new boyfriend, was six-and-a-half feet tall, with muscles the size of watermelons, and belonged to some biker club called the Gold Vipers. I'd only met him twice and I had to admit, he scared the hell out of me. Not that he'd been anything but cordial. It was just that I could tell he was dangerous.

As in *illegally-scary*, dangerous.

Krystal didn't seem to see it or else she just didn't care. Considering her dad took off many years ago and Bonnie, her mom, had never been very influential when it came to *anything*, I guessed it was the latter.

"I wonder if he has something for me?" said Krystal, her blue eyes lighting up. "A present."

"What, like a ring?" I teased. They'd only gone out a few times, and most of their dates were quick hook-ups.

"Or better yet, a new tongue ring," she replied. "You have any idea how good a pierced tongue feels between your legs?"

I held up my hand. "Stop, right there. I haven't had enough to drink to hear about Tank and his tongue."

She giggled. "Well, it's certainly not going to be a ring for my finger. Tank told me last weekend that he was never going to get married. That most of the guys in the club have Old Ladies and kids, but they don't usually go the route of marriage."

I frowned. "What do you mean by an 'Old Lady'?"

"I'm talking about the woman they go home to at night. The ones they live with. Take care of them. Have their kids."

"That's typically called a 'wife'," I said dryly.

"Not in the MC world," she replied. "They have Old Ladies and," she then laid the whopper on me, "they have their club whores." Only she made it sound like "hures."

My jaw dropped. "Are you fucking serious?"

"As shit," she said, smiling grimly.

"A club *whore*? What are you saying? That she hangs out with them and they pay her for sex?"

"I don't think any of them get paid for it. They hang out and are available to fuck, any time of the day."

I stared at her wide-eyed. "Wow. So, in other words, she's like a groupie?"

She laughed. "Guess so. Only these guys ride bikes instead of buses."

"Does Tank have an Old Lady?"

"No. I mean I don't think so." Her jaw set firmly. "At least, I hope to fuck not."

"Well, what are *you* considered?" I asked. "Did he say?"

"He calls me 'his girl'. Tell you one thing, though, I'm definitely not a club whore. The fuck if I'm going to spread my legs for anyone but the man I'm dating. Although," she smiled wickedly, "Tank has this friend named Raptor who is amazingly hot. I wouldn't mind doing him."

"Raptor? What kind of a name is that?" I knew Krystal had mentioned that most bikers went by their road names. All I could think about was the movie *Jurassic Park* when I heard "Raptor."

She grinned. "Raptor? It's some kind of bird of prey. I guess you don't want to piss him off. Tank said that Raptor's temper is legendary."

"Huh. He sounds like someone to avoid. I'd stay away from him then, Krystal. No matter how cute his is."

"You have to see this fucking guy. He's gorgeous. Blonde hair, blue eyes, built like a Greek god. He's unbelievably sexy. I almost wish I would have met Raptor, first. I've actually caught myself drooling over him. Tank would probably pull out his gun and shoot me in the head if I so much as looked at Raptor the wrong way, though."

The expression on her face was serious and I shook my head, still in disbelief. The more she told me about Tank, the more he disgusted me. "Jesus. You're really okay with all of this alpha-male club shit?"

She waved her hand. "Eh, we're just having fun right now. I mean, I like him a lot, don't get me wrong. The guy knows how to go down on a girl and I'm not ready to give that up just yet."

I grunted. "I should have known."

"It's true. He's patient, too. Will stay down there as long as it takes. Anyway, I know it's not going to last. He might have great fucking skills, but Tank's too bossy, even for me."

"God, I hate bossy men. Seriously, Krystal, you shouldn't put up with guys telling you how to live. No matter what he can do with his tongue."

"Yeah, but he's also got this huge dick," she said, laughing. "You have no idea." She held up her hands to show me just how large and I had to wince. "Swear to God, he's hung like a fucking horse."

"Okay, enough," I replied, laughing now. "I'm seriously tired of hearing about your sex life."

"You just need to get laid, Adriana. How long has it been?"

I shrugged. "I don't know, over a year?"

Maybe two.

Maybe even three?

The truth was, I'd only had sex a few times, and that was mostly in high school, when I'd gone steady with Jimmy Tyler. Now that I was in college, I barely had time for sleep, let alone sex.

"We need to remedy that," she said, opening the door. "Let's see what Tank wants, meet the others at the club, and find you a man. One you can take back to the car and fuck the shit out of before the night is over."

I looked around the parking lot, praying that none of the guys entering this particular place would know she was trying to get me laid. "Krystal," I whispered loudly. "Don't announce it here, for God's sake."

She giggled. "Fine, but we're finding you a guy tonight."

Her eyes were sparkling from the schnapps and I could tell she was already quite buzzed. "I don't need a man and this party is for *you*. In fact, I'm not drinking much. Maybe a couple of beers. I want you to have fun. It's your birthday. My birthday has come and gone."

"And so did your chance with that bouncer."

I thought about the guy she was talking about. One of the security guards at a nightclub we'd partied at had come on to me, but I'd ignored him. He'd obviously been a player and had probably brought a new girl home every night.

"Tell you what – we'll work on it *after* your party. This is your night and the only person who needs to have fun and get laid, is you. Now, give me your keys and let the games begin."

I handed them over. "I guess I really can't argue with that."

***

When we walked into the strip club, I immediately felt like all eyes were on us. It was exactly how I'd pictured it to be, too – dark, musty, and in need of new carpeting, and not just the flooring. Most of the waitresses looked like they could collect social security, although they were dressed like high school girls. The ones from *their* generation.

Krystal giggled. "These ladies know that the eighties have come and gone? Kind of like their looks."

I smirked. "God, you're a bitch."

"Well, I do like it doggy-style," she joked. "I cannot lie."

I snorted.

The stage was lit up and the place was packed, although most of the customers looked distracted and uncomfortable, which surprised me. In fact, there was so much tension in the air that I felt like we'd walked into something that was about to turn hostile. Then I noticed there were two groups of men eyeing each other from opposite sides of the room. As I looked closer, I also noticed they had different patches on their vests, or cuts, as Krystal liked to call them. Some said Gold Vipers on the back, while the others said Devil's Rangers.

"Where's Tank?" Krystal asked the bouncer, standing just inside of the door. He was as tall as he was wide, bald, and had a long, bushy red beard.

His eyes dropped to her breasts and he licked his lips. "He's in the back room. I'll let him know you're here. You must be Krystal?"

She nodded. "That's right."

"Who's your friend?" he asked, now leering at me. I was glad I'd worn jeans and a loose sweater, although from the way he was looking at my chest, I could have just as well have been naked.

I forced a smile. "I'm Adriana."

"Adriana, huh? You'd best be watching Adriana's back," he said to Krystal with a smirk, his eyes shifting toward the crowd of men also now gawking at us. "Everyone's gonna know you're Tank's, Krystal, but she's without protection."

My eyebrow arched. "Protection?"

"A man. If I were you, I wouldn't go anywhere in this place without Krystal here. You won't like it. Or," he laughed darkly. "Maybe you will."

"I'll stick with Krystal," I mumbled, already feeling dirty.

He pulled out a cell phone and began texting. "Since the Devil's Rangers are here, I advise that you both go and sit down by the bar. Don't talk to anyone, except Misty, the bartender. I'd escort you myself, but there's a meeting in back and I'm not supposed to leave the front door."

"Okay," she answered.

I followed Krystal toward the bar right as Bob Seger began singing about Main Street, which confirmed that we were definitely in a biker bar. Growing up, I'd always associated Fat Bob with Harleys, beer, and Tom Cruise dancing in his underwear. Apparently, I'd be adding strippers with dentures to that list.

"Stay close," said Krystal, looking back at me over her shoulder. "Don't make eye-contact with anyone."

"Right."

The music picked up and everyone's eyes shifted away from us to a woman with long red hair and enormous boobs, who'd just stepped onto the stage. From the look on her face, I could tell she wasn't a bubbly, happy stripper. When she tried to smile, it was more of a pucker. As if she'd just licked a lime.

Krystal chuckled. "She should have used the money she spent on her tits on some Botox. At least she'd look a little more relaxed."

"Uh, seriously, I don't think anyone will notice anything above her collarbone."

"I need a nurse!" hollered one of the customers, standing up and waving cash. "You're giving me a heart-attack, Betty."

Krystal snorted. "Nurse Betty looks like she's going to have one herself, lugging those monsters around."

Betty wore a nurse's uniform and three-inch stilettos that made her legs look like they went all the way up to the clouds. From the way she moved around the stage, it was obvious she'd been doing it for a long time, but had lost interest in it a couple decades ago.

"Men are such pigs," said Krystal, as another guy leaped onto the stage and grabbed the stripper's boobs with both hands. She began to holler and the man's buddies pulled him down, roaring with laughter. I hoped, for her sake, that the bar paid her decent benefits.

"I hope Tank gets out here quickly," I muttered, as we made our way around the back to the bar.

"You waiting for Tank?" asked the bartender, a pretty woman in her thirties. She had long black hair and wore a Harley tank with denim shorts that barely covered her crotch.

"We are. Two light beers, please," said Krystal. She turned to me. "That okay?"

"Yeah," I replied.

Her eyes widened as she looked past me. "Shit," she mumbled under her breath.

I turned and noticed a group of bikers watching us from their table. One of them was bald and had a long scar on the side of his face. He looked like he was in his forties and had some kind of tattoo under his eye. A teardrop. When our eyes met, he smiled, raised two fingers and wagged his tongue between them.

I quickly looked away. "Seriously, what a gross asshole. Does he actually think he'll get lucky doing that?"

"He gets laid all the time, whether a chick wants to or not, I hear. In fact, those guys are Devil's Rangers," said the bartender, sliding our beers over. "Believe me, though, you don't want to have anything to do with them. The only reason they're here is because Slammer needed to talk to Mud, their Prez."

"Who's Slammer?" I asked.

"That's Tank's dad," said Krystal. "The president of the Golden Vipers."

"Yeah," said Misty. Her eyes narrowed. "Shit, looks like you're going to have company. I'd better go and get Tank before that guy steps out of bounds."

When I turned around, I found myself staring into the soulless eyes of the Devil's Ranger who'd been sticking his tongue out like a dipshit. He was almost a foot taller than me and smelled like pot.

"Hey, beautiful," he said in a raspy voice. "You looking for some company?"

I wanted to tell him I'd rather find my company under a rock, now that we were forehead-to-chin, but he was a little frightening up close. "Uh, no," I answered, trying to appear more brave than I felt. "But, thanks." I looked away, hoping he would now *go* away.

He chuckled. "Name is Breaker. Why don't you come and join us at the table?"

"Thanks, but I have a boyfriend," I lied, turning to face him again.

"Good for you," he said, smiling darkly. "That wasn't the answer I was looking for, though."

I really didn't like this guy and he was now seriously pissing me off. "Sorry, but I guess you won't like this answer either. *No*," I said firmly, surprising myself. "I'd rather stay right here and drink this beer with my friend."

"You're kind of bitch, you know that?" he said, his eyes hardening.

I forced myself to smile as sweetly as possible when I noticed the vein throbbing in his forehead. He looked like he was about ready to explode. "Sorry. Look, neither of us wants any trouble. We just want to be alone, you know?"

His eyes flickered over Krystal. "You two dykes? Is that it?"

My smile fell. I seriously hated that term and if we were lovers, it wasn't his business anyway. "Not that it's any of your business, but no we are not."

"That's good," he said, undressing me with his eyes again. "A body like yours needs to be fucked by a real man, not a rubber strap-on toy. Although," he laughed, "I wouldn't mind watching you play with one."

I looked at Krystal and said, "Wow."

"Speaking of 'wow'. You ever felt the rumble of an engine between your legs?" he asked, leaning closer to me.

"No," I replied, wondering why I was still answering him.

"Let's go pop that cherry then," he answered. "I'll take you for ride on my Harley that will make your pussy drool."

I burst out laughing. "Oh, my God. Are you really that classy?"

"Anyone walks into a place like this shouldn't expect classy," he said. "That goes for stuck-up bitches, too."

I gritted my teeth and forced myself not to reply. I could tell from his expression that he was hoping I would. Daring me to. I looked toward the entrance, hoping to get the bouncer's attention, but he wasn't at his station.

"We're waiting for Tank," said Krystal in a shrill voice.

He ignored her. "I know Blondie is Tank's. I've already been warned. But, nobody mentioned you, sweetness. You've got no patch either. You're free territory. I say we go do a little exploring."

I laughed, trying to make light of everything, even though I was seething inside. Why couldn't he just leave me alone?

"You like that one, huh? I've got something else for you, too," he said, grabbing his crotch. "Now, drink the rest of your beer and we'll hit the road."

"Do I have to spell it out for you?" I said, totally disgusted. "I'm not interested."

Breaker's nostrils flared. "I don't think you understand who you're talking to."

"An asshole is who I'm talking to," I snapped. "Now, fuck off."

His buddies at the table snickered.

The man's hand snaked out and he grabbed my arm roughly. "You fucking cunt. Let's go. Now."

Krystal sucked in her breath. "Oh, my God."

I pulled my arm away from him in shock. The guy was treating me like one of those whores she had told me about. As big and bad as he looked, nobody treated me like a slut that was up for grabs. "Leave me alone," I said through my clenched teeth. "Before I call the bouncer over here."

He laughed coldly. "The bouncer? Good luck with getting help from that pig."

Before I could respond, two other guys stepped next to us, one being Tank.

Breaker took a step back and crossed his arms over his chest. "Hey, Tank. Looks like the meeting is over, huh?"

"Almost. What's going on, Breaker?" asked Tank, picking at his teeth with a toothpick.

"Just havin' me some fun," said the man, smirking. "You said we should relax and enjoy ourselves. So, that's what I'm trying to do."

"Not with my girl, you're not," said a deep voice.

I turned to find myself staring up at a pair of icy blue eyes and a smile that wasn't meant to be friendly.

Breaker's eye narrowed. "Thought Brandy was your Old Lady, Raptor."

So this was Raptor?

I could see why Krystal found him fascinating. He was certainly good-looking, with his square jaw, full lips, and muscular frame. His blond hair was long and pulled back into a ponytail, exposing his ears, which were both pierced. For some reason, he reminded me of a model I'd seen recently in a pricey cologne ad. I'd been drawn to his eyes, thinking they must have been Photo-Shopped because of the dazzling color. That guy had nothing on Raptor, however. His eyes sparkled like the bluest of tanzanite. Bluer than anything my mother had ever sold, and she was a jeweler. They were so stunning that it was hard to look away.

"You thought wrong," answered Raptor.

"Yeah. That ship has sailed," said Tank, smirking. "And... I wouldn't bring her up anymore."

Raptor slid his arm around my waist and pulled me in tightly. "As I was saying, Breaker... this kitten is mine, so I suggest that you go find your own."

Chapter Two

Raptor

I had to do something with my hands before I grabbed Breaker and killed the bastard, so I pulled the chick against me and gave him a look that said 'fuck you'. He was a complete psycho and had we been alone, I'd have made sure he never touched a woman again. Rumor had it that he'd raped and beaten Slammer's Old Lady's daughter. It was what tonight's meeting was about. But, the Devil's Rangers were denying his involvement. Things were getting ugly in the back of the club, but apparently, they were just as ugly in the front.

"As I was saying, Breaker… this kitten is mine, so I suggest that you go find your own."

Breaker looked at me like we wanted to bash my skull in and I stared back at him, daring him to fucking try it.

***

Adriana

Part of me was annoyed that they were treating me like a possession. The other part liked the way Raptor's arm felt around my waist and the smell of him – leather and a trace of cologne. A good cologne. As I leaned closer to get a better whiff, Raptor looked down and our eyes met.

I laughed nervously. "Uh, new cologne, honey?"

He stared at me for a minute and then his lips twitched, as if he was fighting a smile. He turned away and they continued their testosterone-fueled banter, although, I really wasn't paying much attention. I was too intrigued with the guy holding me. I had to admit, he *was* sexier than hell and I liked the way my breasts molded against his side as he held me in place. Either I was ovulating or Krystal was right, it had been way too long since I'd had sex and the heat he was generating was making me warm in all the right places.

Breaker looked from Raptor and then to me, his eyes narrowing. "If she's yours, I'd suggest you patch her before someone snatches her up," he sneered. "Or, better yet, let me know when you're done with her. She might like to know what a real man feels like between her legs."

I felt Raptor stiffen up, but he kept his composure. "Believe me, now that she's had a real man in her honey-hole, your junk would feel more like a sliver off of my timber."

Normally, I would have rolled my eyes at such immature banter, but I had to admit, the thought of Raptor in my honey-hole was interesting.

"I suggest you remember who you're talking to, Raptor," he said, clenching his jaw. "And show some fucking respect."

"You are the last person who should be preaching about respect. You make a move on my woman and then bust *my* chops? What the fuck?" he replied.

"He got you there," said Tank, stepping closer to us. It was obvious he was now getting annoyed with the situation and he was definitely a force to be reckoned with. The guy was built like the Incredible Hulk. "Listen, the meeting is almost over, so I suggest you go and enjoy the show. Delilah is up next and she's not only available, but willing to party after the performance."

Breaker looked at me again and smiled. "I'll be seeing you again, sweetness. I promise. " Then he walked away, his gang watching us carefully from their tables, all of them giving us the stink-eye.

"Fucking worms," mumbled Tank, staring back at the table. "Every last one of them."

"I'm so glad you showed up," said Krystal. "That guy wouldn't take 'no' for an answer. I thought he was going to drag Adriana out of the bar there for a second."

27

"You and me both," I said, shuddering at the thought. Even looking at him now, I could tell the thought wasn't too far from his mind.

"We should probably take both the girls somewhere in back," suggested Tank. "Before Breaker finds some liquid courage at the end of that bottle he's drinking. When he's drunk, he's as mean as he is stupid."

"He should be taught a fucking lesson," said Raptor, still glaring at the other group of bikers.

"I agree but, we can't. Besides, the old man might be giving us the thumbs up to deal with him later, *if* you know what I mean."

Raptor relaxed. "True. Okay, let's go."

"Where we going?" I asked, finishing my beer.

"I'll show you," said Raptor. Then, before I could do anything about it, he picked me up, threw me over his shoulder, and slapped my ass. Hard.

"Hey!" I hollered as he carried me toward the back of the bar. It felt like my butt-cheeks were on fire. "What in the hell are you doing? That hurt. Put me down!"

"Sorry, darlin'," he said, a smile in his voice. He caressed my butt, sending warm tingles into my pelvis. "Does this feel better?"

"Quit touching my ass and put me down," I hissed. "Now."

***

Raptor

I smiled, enjoying not only her reaction, but the way her ass felt under my palm. It was deliciously round and firm. I had to force myself not to keep squeezing it. I had to admit, she was a hot little number. I could see why Breaker wanted her. My dick was already half-cocked at the thought of fucking her now myself. I headed toward the back of the club, to the break-room. I knew Tank wanted to fuck Krystal before she headed out and so I'd have a few minutes of alone time with the brunette. From the way she was staring at me earlier, I could tell she was definitely interested. I wondered if she'd be interested in getting on her knees and opening that sweet little mouth. The thought of her glossy pink lips wrapped around my cock was enough to try and test those salty waters.

***

Adriana

We went through a hallway and he kicked one of the doors open.

"What is your fucking problem?" I snapped. "Are you even listening to me?"

He dropped me into an oversized recliner and took a step back. "You're welcome."

I glared up at him. "For what? Treating me like a cave-woman?"

He grunted and smiled. "Cave-woman? Look, I had to do that. To show everyone in the place that you're mine, Kitten."

Kitten?

"But, I'm *not* yours."

"You know what the fuck I mean. You should be thankful that I did what I did."

"I've had guys flirt with me before. I don't need your help telling them to get lost."

He waved his thumb toward the doorway. "That bastard who was trying to get in your pants is a fucking animal. Hell, he's worse than an animal. He would have taken you somewhere later, then beaten and raped your ass if I wouldn't have helped you. And when I say rape your ass, I'm not just talking figuratively. He would have torn it to shreds."

I stared at him in horror. "Krystal or the bartender would have called the cops if he'd have tried doing something like that."

"The cops wouldn't have done shit," he answered. "In fact, it would be all over before Krystal had a chance to do anything and Breaker wouldn't leave any witnesses. Hell, Krystal is in just as much danger as you."

I sucked in my breath. "Are you saying he'd have killed us?"

"It wouldn't be the first time. They don't call him 'Breaker' for nothing. It should be pronounced 'Break Her'."

"Oh."

"Oh is right," he replied, walking over to an old refrigerator humming in the corner of the room. He opened it up and began rummaging through it. "Dammit, someone's been drinking my beer."

"You keep your own stock of beer in the break room?"

"Sometimes. When I find out who's been helping themselves, I'm going to kick their ass."

"So, back to that guy, Breaker. Has he served time before?"

"Yeah. For assault and rape."

I swallowed.

"So, do you want a beer?" he asked, holding out a brown bottle.

I looked at the dragon tattoo on his forearm and the skull ring on his finger, reminding me that Raptor wasn't exactly the boy-next-door either. "No. We have to get going. Uh, where's Krystal and Tank?" I asked, looking toward the doorway. Obviously, they hadn't followed us.

He grunted. "I'm sure he has her bent over his old man's desk. Giving her a private birthday gift."

I sighed. "Great. I guess we'll be here longer than I thought."

"Yup." He opened up his bottle of beer and took a swig. "You sure you don't want one?" he asked, licking his lips. "It'll give you something to do."

I sighed. "Sure, I'll take one."

He opened up the refrigerator again, and pulled out another bottle.

"So, what, you're going to babysit me?" I asked as he handed me the beer.

"Yeah, you want to sit on my lap, little girl?" he asked, winking at me. "I'll read you a couple of stories. You ever hear the one about Moby Dick?"

My eyes widened. "Is that how you pick up girls? Seriously?"

"Who said I was trying to pick you up?" he answered with a cocky grin. "I was just trying to lighten the mood. You seem a little tense."

"I'm not," I lied.

He sat down on a beat-up leather sofa that faced the television, which was as old as the shag carpeting. "Relax and have a seat," he said, patting the cushion next to him.

"I'm fine," I said, setting my purse on the counter by the coffee machine. I looked around the room. There was a metal table in the corner and a vending machine. "So this is the break-room," I said, trying to make conversation.

"That's what they call it. How old are you, by the way?"

"Twenty-one."

His eyes traveled down the length of me and back up. I knew he was checking me out and it made me wonder if he approved or thought I wasn't curvy enough. I'd always felt a little self-conscious around Krystal, who filled out her bra better than most strippers with silicone.

"How old are *you*?" I asked, resisting the urge to cross my arms over my chest.

"Twenty-four."

"Oh."

He smiled. "Have you ever been to a joint like this?"

"No. Never."

"What do you think of it?"

I smiled. "What do I think? Honestly, I can't wait to leave. No offense."

"None taken. Do you have a boyfriend?"

"Not right now. What about you?"

"No boyfriend, either."

I chuckled. "You know what I mean."

"Yeah, I do," he replied, still not answering the question.

"You're not going to answer?"

He rubbed his lower lip with his index finger. "Why do you want to know?"

My eyes widened. "I don't know. Why did you ask me?"

"To find out if there was a dumbass in your life that allowed you into a place like this."

I stared at him in surprise. "Allowed? I can go wherever the hell that I want. Even if I had a boyfriend, I wouldn't ask for his permission to go into a strip joint or any other place, for that matter."

He grinned. "I am woman. Hear me roar, huh?"

"Damn right," I said, smiling back. I raised my hand and clawed the air. "Roar."

Raptor laughed. "I like that."

"You like independent women?"

"I just like what you did, there. It was sexy. You really are a kitten."

I blushed.

"I mean, I do like independent women, to a point."

"What do you mean, to a point?" I asked.

"I like a woman who can take care of herself when she needs to, but is willing to let a man take care of her when he wants to."

I kind of liked that. To a point. "So, you're not as chauvinistic as Tank?"

"Tank and I agree on some stuff. Some things we don't. It's not like we sit around talking about shit like that."

I smiled. "Yeah, I'm sure you don't."

"So, where are you ladies going tonight?" he asked, changing the subject.

"Clubbing."

"Just you two?"

"No. There are more of us."

"Girls or guys?"

"Just us girls. We all grew up together. Went to the same high school."

"What about protection?"

I frowned. "What do you mean by protection?" *Was he talking condoms?*

He tilted his head, smiling. "You gotta bodyguard chaperoning you little girls, Kitten?"

"We don't need a bodyguard," I said. "And we're not *little* girls." *Nor was I a damn cat.*

"Figure of speech, although, you're pretty small." He took another drink of his beer and licked his lips, studying me. "If you were mine, I wouldn't let you out of the house without some kind of protection. Not with the Devil's Rangers in town. Especially, not after what that asshole said to you earlier."

"I'm not worried," I answered, now a little unsure myself. "It's not like we're going to the kind of places those guys hang out."

"Maybe. Maybe not. I wouldn't take any chances. Just watch your back tonight. You got a blade hiding in that purse of yours?"

I stared at him in surprise. "A blade?"

"Obviously you don't," he said. "You carrying any mace?"

"No. I don't even know where to get mace."

"A goddamn whistle, at the very least?"

I smirked. "Why, so that I can call a *Time Out?*"

He grunted. "I'm not trying to be funny. How about a cell phone?"

I nodded toward my purse. "Yeah. Of course."

He stood up and walked over to it.

"What are you doing?"

He unzipped the top and began rummaging through it. "Jesus, how much stuff can one girl carry around in here?" he asked, waving a tampon. "Got your friend, huh? This is probably a good deterrent. Try waving it in the air if you run into trouble. Nobody will mess with your shit. Believe me."

"Seriously?" I said quickly, snatching it from him. "I don't have my period. Not that it's any of *your* business. That's for emergencies. Would you *please* get out of my purse," I said, pulling it away from him just as he found my phone.

"I'm going to add my name and phone number to your contacts list. You get into any trouble tonight or," he smiled wickedly, "interested in hooking up later, call me."

Something told me that hooking up with him would be the death of me, as hunky as he was. I would never have the guts to call him or find out what was hidden under his low-riding jeans anyway. "I don't do hook-ups."

He pushed some buttons on my phone. "Why, you need to be wined and dined first?"

I blushed. "Maybe."

"Fair enough." He grinned. "How do you feel about wine and wings at my apartment later?"

I raised my eyebrow. "Really? You wouldn't even buy me a real dinner? Just an appetizer?" He opened his mouth to say something, but I interrupted him. "Please don't tell me that you're the main course or that you have a large tube-steak for me, either."

He laughed and handed me my phone. "I don't need to use a line like that to get laid."

"Good, because we both know that it would be extremely tacky."

Before he could reply, a noise from one of the nearby rooms caught our attention. The sound began to increase and I quickly recognized it as Krystal's cries of pleasure.

"Looks like your friend is a screamer," said Raptor, turning around. He leaned back against the counter and took another swig of beer. "Good thing the meeting is upstairs in the back, or there'd be hell to pay. Slammer doesn't like distractions. Especially when he's not the one involved in it."

I rubbed my forehead as the sounds grew louder. I couldn't tell if hearing the other couple getting it on was embarrassing, or just making Raptor that much more appealing. "Maybe I should just go wait out in the car for her."

"Maybe you should just finish your beer and stay inside here with me. Where you're safe."

From the way he was smiling, his definition of 'safe' contradicted mine.

Chapter Three

Raptor

Holy shit was my dick begging to come out and play. I had more wood than Yellowstone National Park. It wasn't just the noises in the other room that were making me horny, either. It was *her*. Sure, she was beautiful, with those come-fuck-me emerald eyes and that chestnut colored hair that I knew would feel good in my fist when I was banging her from behind. But it wasn't only that. It was something else that was starting to suck me in and I couldn't put my finger on it.

"Looks like your friend is a screamer," I said, leaning back against the counter after hearing Krystal scream again. I took another swig of beer. "Good thing the meeting is downstairs or there'd be hell to pay. Slammer doesn't like distractions. Especially when he's not the one involved in it."

She rubbed her forehead as the sounds grew louder. "Maybe I should just go wait out in the car for her."

I smiled wickedly. "Maybe you should just finish your beer and stay inside here with me. Where you're safe."

From the look on her face, she knew that she was far from being safe. Something told me she didn't care, either. That she was intrigued. If she even looked at my crotch with interest, I'd be on her like a dog in heat, which truthfully, was probably a bad idea since Adriana was the kind of girl I normally tried to avoid. The kind that went to college, went to church, and didn't fuck on the first date. The kind that needed monogamy and commitment. I was down with that before Brandy had fucked me over. But, she'd taught me a lesson. Never trust anyone but your brothers. Not even the woman who warms your bed at night and sucks your dick until dawn. She's always looking for someone else to replace you. Someone with a bigger wallet or a bigger dick. Apparently, in my case, it was a bigger wallet since Brandy had started calling me back, wanting to hook up since her boss wasn't making her come the way I had. Still, knowing that this chick wasn't like Brandy, or the rest of the whores that usually hung around the club, made me want to bury myself deep inside of her that much more.

Look at my crotch.
Come on, Kitten.
I dare you.

***

Adriana

"Safe, huh?" I replied as Krystal howled in pleasure.

"Have to admit, listening to those two is getting me a little jacked up. I haven't had sex for a while and this isn't helping," he said. "What about you?"

"What *about* me?"

"Are you horny, baby?" he joked, mimicking Austin Powers.

I stared at him in surprise. "Of course not."

"Liar," he said softly, smiling. "Your face is flushed."

"That's because I'm creeped out."

"Sex creeps you out?"

"No," I said a little sharply. "I just don't care to hear other people having it."

His eyes traveled over my body. "We could remedy that fairly easily."

"Oh, yeah? How?"

He grinned. "Drown out their noises with ours."

I laughed. "Wow. Seriously?"

"When it comes to sex? Yeah," he said.

I shook my head and smiled. "I don't think I've ever met anyone as forward as you. Do you flirt like this with all the girls you meet?"

"Not girls like you."

"What do you mean, girls like me?"

He paused. "Classier ones."

His compliment made me smile. "So, what are you saying? That you usually only flirt with unclassy ones?" I joked, feeling a little flattered but nervous, too.

"Actually, I don't have to flirt with them. They usually come on to me."

"So, do you usually prefer the skanks?"

He smirked. "Those I usually prefer on their knees."

I laughed. "But not the classy ones?"

"Then, I'm usually the one on my knees."

My face turned scarlet at that image.

He bit his lower lip and smiled "Sorry, am I embarrassing you?"

"You're making it a little... awkward."

"Sorry. Ever since I saw you blushing earlier, I couldn't help myself. I wanted to see it again. It's damn cute."

There was a thud from the room next door. Then another and another, until it became a steady rhythm.

"Looks like they've graduated to the bed. Hopefully, they'll be done soon," he said as the noises grew louder.

"Wow, they have a bed in there, huh?" I said as Krystal's moans seeped through the wall. I knew it was her birthday, but this was getting ridiculous.

"Of course. Only Tank and his dad use it, though."

"Not you?"

"I've never used it. I have higher standards when it comes to sex."

"Bars aren't your thing?"

"Other men's beds are not my thing."

"I don't blame you. So, how do you know Tank?" I asked, trying to change the subject.

"We're brothers."

I pulled my hair over my shoulder and stared at him in surprise. "Really? I didn't know he had one."

"We're all brothers here," he said, taking another swig of beer.

"Ah."

"Ah?"

"I get it. You're *biker* brothers."

He smirked. "You think you've figured us out, huh? I bet you're from the suburbs and have no idea what it's like, being on your own."

"Maybe not, but I heard that Tank is also from the suburbs," I said, feeling a little defensive.

"Yeah, but it's different for him. He's lived the MC life since he was born. Obviously, you don't know what that shit entails. But if you did, you'd understand where I'm coming from. Your parents probably sheltered you your entire life, which I can't blame them. If I had a daughter, I'd want to do the same thing. Keep you safe."

"I'm not sheltered," I replied stiffly.

He smirked. "Believe me, you're sheltered. You have no idea what's really going on out there, Kitten. On the streets and, hell, in your own backyard, now. Drugs, prostitution, sex-trafficking, murder."

"I watch the news," I said. "I know what's out there. I've even taken self-defense classes."

"Self-defense classes?" he repeated, looking amused. "What kind?"

"Just some basic stuff. How to knock a knife out of someone's hand. Kick him in the junk. Things like that."

"You think if I came at you, you'd be able to defend yourself against me?" asked Raptor, setting his beer down.

"It's easier to defend myself against someone who isn't ready for me to fight back."

"Actually, those scumbags will anticipate you trying to defend yourself in one way or another. Why don't you show me what you've learned?"

"No, that's okay," I said, staring up at him now. He'd moved closer and the thought of him putting his arms around me was making my heart race.

"Come on. Don't be frightened. I'll be gentle."

"I'd really rather not," I said, as he moved closer.

"I think you should," he said. He was so close, I could smell the beer on his breath. "If you girls are going out by yourselves, and drinking, you should definitely know how to defend yourself."

"I don't want to hurt you," I said, keeping my beer between us.

He laughed. "I don't think there's any chance of that."

"Don't be too sure," I said, looking down at my brown leather ankle-boots. They had narrow heels and I imagined if I kicked him the way my instructor had shown me, it would wipe the smile right off of his face.

Before I could stop him, he grabbed my beer and set it on the counter. "Come here," he said, pulling me toward the middle of the room.

"I just told you I didn't want to do this," I protested.

"Humor me. Please," he said, turning around to face me. "I just want to see what these classes teach and maybe even give you some more pointers."

"Fine," I said with a sigh. "But, just don't get mad if I hurt you."

"I'll try not to," he said, his mouth twitching.

"Okay," I answered, trying to recall all of the things my instructor, Mr. Mandrill, had taught me. "So, um, whenever you're ready."

"What do you want me to do?"

I waved my hand. "I don't know. You're the one who wanted to see me defend myself. I guess if you were going to attack a woman, do what you'd do."

"Me? If I was going to attack a woman, it would be in bed and not on the streets," he said, smiling wickedly. "And I doubt she'd fight back."

I rolled my eyes. "Whatever, Casanova. Just attack me. In fact, I'll turn and you can try to get me from behind."

"Now we're talking," he answered, a smile in his voice, as I turned my back on him.

"Okay. Whenever you're ready."

"Okay," he said, wrapping his arms around me so quickly that I barely had time to exhale. He held my wrists together in front of me. "Show me what you got, Kitten."

I hesitated for a second, enjoying the feel of his chest pressing against my back and the heat his body was generating. And, was it my imagination, or was there something hard pressed against my ass?

"You smell good," he whispered near my ear. "I think you'd better free yourself before I forget why we were doing this."

I felt a warm shiver go through me as I imagined his lips on my neck and then other parts of my body.

"Well?"

I stomped on his foot with my heel and he let me go, hollering in pain.

"Oh, my God!" I cried as he bent over to rub the top of his boot. "I'm so sorry!"

I heard a door slam and then Tank was rushing into the room, shirtless. "What the fuck is going on in here?"

"Nothing. It's okay," said Raptor, putting his foot down.

"What's wrong with your foot?" said Tank as Krystal entered the room, adjusting her clothes.

"I did it," I said, feeling my face turn red.

Raptor removed his black boot and then his sock. "But, I forced her into it," he said, staring down at his foot, which was already bruising up. "Damn, girl, those heels are deadly."

"I'm sorry," I repeated, still feeling horrible. "I did warn you, though."

"I know you did."

"*You* did that?" asked Krystal, walking over to get a better look. "How?"

"I was pretending to attack her and she stopped me," said Raptor. "Good move, by the way."

"Thanks," I said, smiling sheepishly. "Uh, I really am sorry."

He put his sock back on. "It'll heal. I've been through much worse."

"Can you walk?" asked Tank.

He took a couple steps. "Of course. See. Hell, I could probably still kick your ass with it without flinching."

Tank snorted. "Yeah, you wish. It doesn't look so good to me. I'll go get you a stiff drink. Come on, Krystal, walk with me, babe."

"Uh, okay," she said and looked back at me. "I'll be right back and then we'll get going."

"Sure," I said. I turned back to Raptor, who was attempting to put his boot back on. "Do you think I broke anything?"

"No," he replied, wincing.

"Maybe you should have that looked at," I said, staring at his foot.

"Seriously, it's okay, Kitten. Don't worry about me."

I laughed and shook my head.

"What's so funny?"

"You keep calling me Kitten."

He winked. "What can I say, I like kittens. I especially like it when they curl up around your face to stay warm. Something tells me I'd like you there, too."

"By your face?"

"On my face."

I gasped, my face turning scarlet.

He laughed. "Sorry, I just love to see you blush, darlin'."

We stared at each other for a few seconds and then I asked him where he was from.

"I have a house a few blocks away."

"You live there alone?"

His eyes narrowed. "Why are you asking if I live alone?"

"I'm just curious. You don't have to tell me if you don't want to," I said, noticing the guarded look in his eyes. "I was just making conversation."

He relaxed. "Sorry. Yeah, I live alone. Most of the time. Sometimes I take in teens who need a temporary place to stay."

I stared at him in surprise. I wasn't expecting that. "What? You're kidding?"

"No. Not at all. I do some volunteering at one of the shelters in Barnesfied. Sometimes, when they get a little over-run with families, I volunteer my extra bedrooms. Sometimes."

"Wow."

"Shocked, huh? You shouldn't judge people, Kitten. I don't know if I should smile at your surprise or be offended."

"I'm sorry. It just seems out of character for a guy in a... motorcycle gang like yours."

His eyes hardened. "Most of the guys in our club have families and kids of their own. They're good people."

"I'm sorry. I didn't mean anything by it."

"Maybe not, but you were stereotyping."

I smiled grimly. "Yeah, I guess I was."

He sighed. "I lived on the streets most of my life growing up. My old man was an asshole and kicked me out of the house when I was thirteen. That's when Slammer took me in. I owe him my life and I want to make a difference in someone else's if I get the chance. Kids aren't meant to be thrown out like garbage."

"Why did your dad kick you out?"

He was quiet for a few seconds and then sighed. "He used to beat my mom. I tried stopping him one night. He didn't like it."

"So he kicked you out?"

He grunted. "Yeah, after he beat the hell out of me."

My jaw dropped. "That must have been horrible. And you were only thirteen?"

"An 'old' thirteen, believe me."

"What happened to your mom?"

"She ended up in the hospital. When she got out, I heard she packed her bags and disappeared."

"She didn't try to find you?"

"She knew where I was. I guess she just wanted to run away from everything," he said. "At least that's what she put in the letter she left me. She trusted Slammer to watch over me."

"She knew him?"

He stared at his beer. "She used to be a club whore."

I sucked in a breath.

His eyes met mine. "It wasn't for this club. A different one. The one my dad belonged to."

I wasn't sure what to say so I waited for him to continue.

"After she got pregnant with me, he took her in and made her his Old Lady. I don't think he wanted to, though. It's probably why he was such an asshole to her."

"He was an asshole to you, too, though. And you were his son."

He smirked. "Guess he didn't want a son, either."

I almost missed the look of pain in his eyes because it disappeared so quickly. "So, Slammer took you in?"

"Yep." He smiled. "He's definitely the shit and I'd do anything for him. Made me his Road Captain a few years ago."

"What does that mean?"

"I'm in charge of trips," he said. "Among other things."

I stared at the small patches on the front of his black leather cut. "What does that one-percent stand for?"

He looked down. "It's symbolizes something the club believes in."

"And what is that?" I asked when he didn't elaborate.

"Have you ever heard anyone use the term 'outlaw biker'?"

"Outlaw? No." My eyes widened. "Is there a warrant out for your arrest or something?"

"No." He scratched his chin and chucked. "At least, I hope not."

"I still don't get what the one-percent stands for and what it has to do with being an outlaw."

It took him a while to answer. "It means that we're committed to standing behind our brothers and living the biker lifestyle. Our laws aren't exactly the same ones that the other ninety-nine percent follow. Because of that, we're often labeled as being outlaws."

"Oh," I replied. "You're basically like a biker kind of mafia?"

Before he could answer, Tank stepped back into the room with Krystal.

"You ready to go?" she asked.

I nodded.

"I'm sending Bull with you," said Tank. "Make sure you girls aren't harassed tonight."

"We don't need a chaperone," said Krystal. "I already told you that."

"This is for protection. It's not for babysitting you," he said.

"I don't care. I don't want anyone tagging along. It will be embarrassing," she said, pouting.

Tank's jaw clenched. "Fine. Have it your way."

"Don't be angry," she said, standing on her tippy-toes to kiss him. "Where we're going, there won't be any bikers. Seriously. Plus, Adriana knows self-defense."

"She certainly does," said Raptor, nodding toward his foot. "She can probably take Bull out."

Tank grunted. "I doubt that. Fine, babe. You run into any problems, though, you call me. Pronto."

"I will. I promise," she said, kissing his lips.

"I'll walk you out to the car," said Tank. We'll go out the back, so those dirt-bags don't see you leaving."

"Okay," said Krystal, putting her purse around her shoulder. "Ready, Adriana?"

I nodded.

"You girls have fun," said Raptor. "And call me if you change your mind about having that pizza, later, Kitten."

Krystal looked at me, her eyebrows raised.

"Right," I said, smirking.

"Let's go," said Tank, walking out the door.

She grabbed my arm as we followed him. "Kitten?" she whispered.

"Apparently he likes cats."

"Bullshit. What he likes is pussy," said Tank, laughing in front of us.

Chapter Four

Adriana

We arrived at Rumors, a club in Iowa City about twenty minutes later. The music was loud and the dance-floor, which was the size of a football field, was packed. By the time we found our friends, Monica, Tiffany, and Amber, they were already tipsy.

"Where've you been?" asked Monica, who was a year older than us. "We were getting worried."

"We stopped off at Griffin's," said Krystal, sliding in next to her. "Tank had to give me his birthday gift."

"What was that? A frosted cock?" said Tiffany, who was a nympho, like Krystal. "Did you blow out his candle?"

"No, I waxed it pretty good, though," she said, giggling.

Tiffany laughed. "You go, girl!"

"And lucky me. I got to hear the whole thing," I said dryly. "The walls in that dump are pretty thin."

"At least you were able to spend some time with Raptor," she said. "You have to admit, he's hot."

"Yeah. He's also a biker, and not the kind who's into triathlons. I don't care how hot a guy like that is, he's trouble."

Krystal leaned forward. "He's worth the trouble, if you ask me. Speaking of which, I overheard some stuff about the Devil's Rangers. Remind me to tell you about it."

"Like I care about those freaks," I said, thinking back to Breaker. The nerve of that jerk ordering me around. It left a bad taste in my mouth. As far as I was concerned, I was never going back to Griffin's.

A waitress stopped at our table carrying a tray of shot glasses. "Hi. The guys over there just bought you a round of raspberry-flavored Kamikazes."

We turned to look at the table she was talking about. There were four guys smiling at us, all of them looked like they'd just stepped out of GQ Magazine.

"Now that's what I'm talking about," said Tiffany, blowing them a kiss.

Krystal raised her shot. "Thank you!" she hollered.

I waved my hand and so did Amber.

"Aren't they yummy?" said Tiffany, after we made a toast to Krystal's birthday and sucked down the delicious concoction. "The guys, I mean."

"They're cute," I agreed, noticing one of them staring at me. When he saw me looking, he smiled widely, and took a drink of his beer.

"I'll bet they're frat boys," said Tiffany. "We should go over and talk to them."

"No. Let them come to us," said Krystal.

My eyebrows rose. "Listen to you. What about Tank?"

She sighed. "You know, to be honest, I'm kind of bored with him."

"You didn't sound too bored earlier," I said.

"I know but… oh look, they're coming over," she answered, smiling.

I turned to find myself staring up at the guy who'd been eyeballing me. He certainly was cute, but for some reason, I wasn't half as attracted to him as I had been to Raptor, which was kind of weird. Normally, I preferred clean-cut and safe. Raptor was neither.

"Hi," he said. "I'm Jason and that's Gary, Lucas, and Brian."

"Thanks for the shots. They were yummy," said Krystal, staring at Lucas with interest. She introduced us to them.

Lucas, who was blonde and had dimples, smiled. "No problem. Would you like more?" he asked, reaching for his wallet.

"That depends – are you trying to get us drunk?" asked Tiffany, smiling slyly.

Lucas gave her a horrified look. "No. Not at all. I hope you don't think that."

She laughed. "Chill out. I'm just teasing you."

He relaxed. "Would you like a soda?"

"Hell no. I'm here to get drunk!" she shouted, slapping her hand on the table.

He laughed. "Alrighty, then."

I could tell by his expression that he didn't know what to make of Krystal but was certainly enjoying her cleavage.

"Where are you girls from?" asked Jason, staring at me intently.

"Jensen," I said.

"All of you?" asked Brian, who was the shortest out of the group, even shorter than me and I was five-seven. He was built like a wrestler, though. All muscle. Even his neck.

"Yes," said Krystal. "We all went to high school together."

"They sure know how to grow them in Jensen," said Gary, who looked a little drunk. He was tall, lanky, with big brown eyes and a boyish smile. "Must be the fertilizer."

Jason patted Gary on the back. "Excuse our friend, it's his birthday and we've been buying him shots. Quite a few of them."

"It's my birthday, too," said Krystal, beaming a smile at Gary. "From the look of things, I think I need to try catching up to you!"

"Hey, happy birthday... what wuss your name again?" asked Gary, trying to focus.

"Krystal."

"Krystal? What a beautiful name. I'll bet you even smell like a flower." His eyes dropped to her chest. "Like a 'Krystal Of The Valley'."

"That's Lily Of The Valley," said Jason, shaking his head.

"Oh, she knows what I mean," he said, still staring at her chest. "I love them valleys."

She laughed. "Looks like you love hills, too."

Gary burst out laughing. "That's right."

"Okay, Romeo," said Brian. "Try to roll your tongue back into your mouth before someone trips over it on the dance floor."

Gary ignored him. "Hey. Krystal, the Birthday Girl. Lemme buy you a drink. Waitress!" he hollered, swaying. "Waitress?"

"Maybe you should let us order it," said Jason, squeezing his shoulder. "They'll cut you off if they notice how drunk you are."

Gary shrugged him off. "I'm not drunk. Jus' feeling real good. Come on, man."

"Settle down, Gary," said Lucas, who'd been pretty quiet up until then.

"You settle down," slurred Gary. "You're embarrassing yourselves."

Lucas grunted.

"So, where are you guys from?" asked Tiffany, trying to divert the conversation.

"We go to school at I.U.," said Jason.

"Iowa University?" asked Monica.

"Yep," said Gary, standing up straighter. "We're frat brothers."

"Which fraternity?" I asked. I was currently working on my Associate's Degree in Accounting, and also attended I.U. I knew how crazy some of those guys could get.

Gary was about to answer when Brian interrupted. "Aren't you with Delta Epsilon?" he asked Krystal. "I swear I've seen you at one of their rallies."

"No," she answered, smiling brightly. "I've already finished school."

"She's a Cosmetologist," said Monica. "We graduated Waverly Beauty School together."

Brian ran a hand over his short, spiky hair. "I might have to come and visit you soon then. Which salon do you work at?"

"Shear Images, over in Jensen," she replied. "I'd love to do your hair."

"I'd love you to 'do' my hair," he said, his smile flirtatious.

"Why don't you two just do each other?" said Gary, smiling drunkenly.

Brian sighed. "Sorry. He's not usually like this."

"Don't worry," she answered. "We all have one of those kinds of friends, right, Tiffany?"

Tiffany, who had gotten so drunk on my birthday that she'd flashed all of the bartenders at a different club, before puking in the bathroom, smiled and flipped her off.

"She did get us some free shots, though," I said, laughing.

"Exactly," replied Tiffany. "And I didn't flash them because I was drunk. I flashed them because one of you dared me."

"Yeah, never dare Tiffany anything," said Monica. "Unless you're prepared to see it actually happen."

"I like brave women. So, what do we get, since we've already bought you shots?" asked Gary, now leering at Tiffany's chest. "A little peek of those peaks?"

Tiffany looked at me and rolled her eyes.

I just shook my head and laughed.

"You sure know how to win over the ladies," said Jason dryly, taking another drink of his beer.

"Oh, I'm just having some fun," he replied. "You know that, right, Terry?"

"It's Tiffany," she corrected.

"That's right, Tiffany. Hey, waitress!" he said, waving his arms. "Over here!"

The server made her way over and the guys bought us another round of drinks.

"I'll have a rum and Coke, please," I told the waitress and then looked at Krystal. "Then I'm done. I'm driving, remember."

"We could take a cab," she said. "Then you don't have to worry about it."

"Or, one of us could drive you home," said Jason.

I shook my head. "No, it's okay. I'm not much of a drinker, anyway."

"Has anyone ever told you that you look like that actress, what's her name…" said Gary, snapping his fingers at me. "Oh, yeah – Eva Longoria?"

"I tell Adriana that all the time," said Krystal. "But she doesn't believe me."

"You do look like her," agreed Jason. He smiled. "Maybe her younger, prettier sister."

Gary laughed. "Now if that doesn't sound like a line, I don't know what does! Eva Longoria is a fucking babe, although so are you," he said, leaning toward me. "Seriously, you have the same kind of eyes, too. Are your parents Mexican or Latino?"

"My mother is Portuguese," I said.

"Oh, that explains your exotic look," he replied.

"My exotic look?" I replied, raising my eyebrows.

He nodded. "Yeah. You know – you've got that honey colored skin and, those green eyes of yours… they're like a cat's. You must get asked out all the time."

"Not really," I said.

"I don't believe that for a second," said Jason.

"She just got hit on at Griffin's," said Krystal. "We barely made it out of there alive."

"You two were at Griffin's? The strip joint?" said Lucas, waking up.

"Yes," I said. "Unfortunately."

"What were you doing there?" asked Gary. "Stripping?"

I laughed. "No, we were –"

"Looking for a free lap dance," interrupted Krystal. "I heard they give them to you on your birthday. I thought it would be fun."

"Whoa, you chicks are into other girls?" hollered Gary, looking like he was about to have an orgasm right there on the spot. "Lipstick lesbians. Holy shit that's hot!"

59

"We are not lesbians," I replied, amazed that I'd said it twice in one night.

"She's right. We're not. It was another dare," said Krystal, putting her arm around me. "Right, babe?"

I smiled, knowing what she was going to do. She loved messing around with guys. "Right."

Krystal leaned over and kissed my lips. It was quick, but Gary reacted like we'd just had an hour-long make-out session. "Fuck me! Did you guys see that? Do it again, only this time, grab each other's tits."

Tiffany laughed. "Can I get some of that?" she asked, leaning over the table.

"Of course, babe," said Krystal, pressing her lips against Tiffany's.

"Oh, mama… Can *I* get some of that?" joked Brian.

Krystal winked. "If you buy me another shot, I might just forget that you don't have tits and let you."

Brian pulled out his wallet. "What would you like?" he asked, grinning.

She laughed and then said, "Does anyone have to go to the bathroom?"

"I'm going to call Paul," said Amber, holding up her cell phone. She'd been quietly texting. "He's been sending me messages."

"Tell him you're having fun and to leave you alone," said Tiffany.

"Easier said than done," said Amber, scowling. "I'll be back."

"Who's Paul?" asked Gary.

"Her fiancé," I answered, watching as Amber walked away.

"Tiffany? Monica? Adriana? Do any of you need to go to the bathroom?" asked Krystal again.

"Sure. I'll come with you," I replied, grabbing my purse.

"I'm good," said Tiffany.

"Me, too," said Monica. "We'll save our table. It's getting really crowded."

"You need a chaperone?" asked Gary, smiling like a goon again.

"Nope, but good try," said Krystal, grabbing my arm. "We'll be back."

Chapter Five

Adriana

When we reached the bathroom, three girls walked out and it was just the two of us.

"Did you see how riled up Gary got when he thought we were lesbians?" said Krystal, laughing.

"So did Brian. He likes you, you know."

She smiled. "Do you think so?"

"Of course."

"Jason was staring at you. I'm sure he likes you."

"I can't see why. I look like I've been through a tornado," I said, grimacing at my reflection. My hair was all over the place and my makeup definitely needed to be touched-up. I pulled out my brush and began using it.

"Sorry. I should have told you. It's been like that ever since Raptor threw you over his shoulder. What was that like?"

"What was what like?"

"Having that gorgeous creature carry you into the back room. For a minute there, I thought you two were going to go at it."

My eyes widened. "You mean have sex?"

"Yes."

"I don't even know him."

"Who cares? A guy as hot as him has got to be fantastic in bed."

I smiled. "Probably."

"He gave you his number, right?" she said as two girls walked into the bathroom and began talking quietly in the corner about some guy.

"Yes."

"Are you going to use it?"

"No," I said, lowering my voice.

She smiled. "Maybe I should use it."

My jaw dropped. "What would Tank say?"

She shrugged. "I'd make Raptor keep it to himself."

"I doubt it. They've got this bond… He started telling me about it."

"Yeah. I know. They're 'brothers' because of the club," she said as the two girls left the bathroom. "The truth is that I'm pretty sure if I hit on Raptor, Tank wouldn't just break up with me. He'd hunt me down and beat the shit out of me."

"Seriously?"

She smiled grimly. "He's got a temper. They've all got tempers."

"Maybe you should break up with him."

"Like I said earlier, I'm thinking about it." Krystal reached into her purse and pulled out a small white vial of powder. "By the way, Tank scored me some coke for my birthday. You want some?"

My eyes widened in shock. "No. I didn't know you did that shit."

She shrugged. "Just a few times. Tank said this is the really good stuff. Are you sure you don't want to try some? It'll wake you up and make you want to dance all night." She giggled. "It even makes you horny."

I stared at her in disbelief. Where was my friend who used to complain about her mom smoking pot? Now, *she* was snorting coke? "You know I'm not into that crap and I didn't think you were either. Let me guess, Tank is also the one who introduced you to it?"

"Yeah. So? Don't make a big deal out of it," she said, stuffing it back in her purse as someone walked in. She turned around and headed for the largest stall. "Don't go back without me. I'll be done in a minute."

Sighing, I went into the other stall, did my business, and then washed my hands. A few seconds later, Krystal stepped out of her stall and quickly washed her hands. Our eyes met in the mirror and I could see that she was already beginning to feel the effects.

"What?" she asked, frowning.

I just shook my head.

"Don't be a buzz-kill," she replied, pulling at a paper towel. "Seriously."

"Whatever. You know how I feel about it. Anyway, it's your life."

"You're right. It is. Let's go," she replied, walking out of the bathroom.

When we made it back to the table, I noticed that Jason and Tiffany were on the dance floor, their hands all over each other. Thinking he'd been attracted to me, I felt a twinge of disappointment. I brushed it off and concentrated on the drink the waitress had brought, and listening to Gary ramble on about how his girlfriend had left him the week before.

"Your girlfriend left you?" repeated Krystal, knocking her knuckles on the table. "Why?"

"She thinks I have a drinking problem," he said, smiling sheepishly.

Krystal tilted her head and smiled up at him. "Do you?"

He shrugged. "No. Maybe. I don't know. I'm in college. I'm supposed to get drunk and have fun, right?"

"Exactly… I'll drink to that," she said and then quickly drank half of her cocktail. She set it back on the table and shuddered. "Whoa, now that's what I call a good fucking Mai Tai. Hey." She looked at Brian, who was standing next to Lucas and talking about football. "You want to dance?"

"Sure," he said, smiling. He set his drink down and then held out his arm. "Don't hate me if I step on your toes."

She stood up and slid her arm through his. "I'm not worried about it. Monica?" she asked as a new song started, something with a faster beat.

"No, I'm fine right here," she said. Monica hated dancing.

Krystal looked at me and I shook my head.

"I'll dance with you guys," said Gary, setting his drink down as a new song started. "I love this one."

"Okay, Gary. Let's go, boys," said Krystal, holding onto both of them. She looked back over her shoulder as they began walking toward the dance floor. "The rest of you are all a bunch of party poopers!"

We waved at her.

"Have fun!" I hollered.

"Looks like she's been partying enough for all of us," replied Monica, twirling her straw around in her glass.

"Oh yeah," I answered.

"It's her birthday. That's the point, right?" asked Lucas.

"True. Hey, where's Amber?" I asked, as Lucas sat between us.

"She left," they both said at once.

I frowned. "Why?"

Monica shrugged. "I don't know. Something about Paul."

"Oh."

"So, it's just the three of us party poopers" said Lucas, smiling as he leaned back in the chair.

"Why aren't you out there dancing?" I asked.

"Two left feet," he replied. "What about you?"

"I don't know. Just not in the mood, I guess."

He nodded toward my cocktail. "Drink up. I'm sure that will help."

I smiled and picked up the glass. "Thanks for the drinks, by the way."

"No problem. Jason bought this round. You want a shot? I'll get you one."

"No. Like I was saying earlier, I need to be careful. I'm driving."

"Are you always careful?" he asked, his dark eyes sparkling.

I could tell Lucas was flirting with me and he seemed like a nice guy. I just wasn't interested. "When I need to be. Like now."

"Fair enough. What about you?" he asked Monica.

"I have a son. I have to be careful."

I could tell from the look in his eyes that she was marked off of his "To Do" list.

"So, tell us a little about yourself, Lucas," I said, trying not to yawn. It wasn't even eleven and I was already getting bored.

"Not much to tell," he said, looking toward the bar. "Oh shit."

"What's wrong?" I asked, turning to see what he was staring at. There was a girl with two guys ordering drinks at the bar.

He smirked. "Guess you could call her an ex-girlfriend," he said, nodding toward them.

"The girl with the two guys?" I said.

"Yeah. She's completely nuts. If she sees me, she might freak out, which, I guess, is my cue to leave. I'm going to go and find Jason," he said, getting up. "Let him know I'm leaving."

"Okay. Well, it was nice meeting you," I said, feeling bad that his ex was so crazy that he couldn't even be in the same bar with her.

"Yeah," agreed Monica. "Sorry we didn't get a chance to talk more."

"Another time, maybe," he said, looking at the girl again. Then his eyes met mine. He winked. "Enjoy yourself tonight."

"Thanks," I replied.

Still watching the bar, carefully, he took off toward the dance floor, leaving me and Monica alone.

"Boy, that was weird," said Monica. "He's obviously afraid of her."

"She must be a real head-case," I replied.

"You never know. He might just be saying that. We don't know him, either. He could be a real asshole."

"True."

She yawned. "I'm getting tired. I was up with Max early this morning." Max was her five-year-old son. "He wasn't feeling well. I hope I'm not coming down with anything. That's all I need."

"I hear you," I said, taking another drink of my cocktail. "Wow, this is strong."

"Don't drink any more of it then."

I pushed it away. "Maybe I won't."

"I envy you," she said, sighing. "Not that I don't love Max, hell, you know how much I adore that little guy, but there are days when I wish I would have been more careful."

Monica had gotten pregnant in high school and the boy who'd knocked her up, hadn't wanted anything to do with the baby.

"I'm sure. Thank goodness your mom didn't freak out when you first told her about Max."

"She's great. If it wasn't for her, I don't know how I'd have managed."

"You would have found a way. You're a lot more resourceful and independent than you give yourself credit for."

"Thanks," she said. "Still, I wish I could give him more, you know? He deserves it."

"He has his mother," I said, "who loves him and that's all he really needs. You're doing great."

She smiled.

"Plus, look at it this way, you'll still be young when Max is old enough to get into a bar. You can buy him his first drink, and everyone will say what a hot MILF you are."

She laughed. "Right."

"He really is a great kid," I said, thinking about his round little cherub face. "So sweet. You're lucky to have him."

She nodded. "He is sweet. He must take after me because his father is a douche bag."

"Yeah he is," I said, feeling a little dizzy. I put my hand up to my forehead. "Is it hot in here or just me?"

"It's a little hot," she said, looking around. "But look at how many people are crammed into this joint."

"It's packed, alright," said Jason, who was suddenly standing next to me. "And there isn't anywhere to move on the dance floor, there are so many bodies out there now."

"Hey," I said, looking behind him. "Where is Tiffany?"

"She's dancing with Brian, Gary, and your friend now," he said, sitting down next to me. "I needed a break."

"Lucas left," said Monica.

He ran a hand through his dark hair. "Yeah, I ran into him on the way back here."

Monica yawned. "I'm tired. I think I need some caffeine."

"Me, too. I'm feeling a little dizzy anyway." I stuck my fingers in into my drink and grabbed an ice cube. "I knew I should have gone to bed earlier last night," I said, rubbing it on my forehead.

"Drink your rum and Coke," he said, nodding toward the drink. "That will help cool you off."

"No. I'm done," I replied, unzipping my purse to get to my wallet. "I think I'm just going to go and get a plain Coke."

"I'll get it for you," he said, jumping up.

I looked up at him. "No. It's okay. You already bought the drink. I feel bad for wasting it."

He waved his hand. "Are you kidding? Don't worry about it. Would you like a Coke, too?" he asked Monica.

"Yes. Please," she said.

"Okay. I'll be right back," said Jason, walking away.

"He's nice," I said, watching him move around the busy bar, trying to find an available bartender.

"Yeah. He's cute, too."

I nodded and closed my eyes.

"You okay?" she said.

I opened my eyes. "Like I said before, I'm a little dizzy."

"There's a lot of stuff going around," she said. "Flu season, you know."

I scowled. "I hope it's not that. Last time I had the flu I couldn't get out of bed for three days."

"You and me both," she said.

Jason returned a few minutes later and handed us our sodas.

"Thanks," I said. "I think I really need this."

"Yeah, thanks," said Monica, taking her soda.

"No problem," he answered, sitting down next to me.

"I'll be right back. I need to go to the bathroom," said Monica, standing up.

"Do you want me to come with you?" I asked.

"No. I'm fine. I'm going to call my mom, too. See how Max is doing."

"Okay," I said, as she walked away.

"So, what do you normally do for fun?" he asked, watching me as I took another drink of the soda.

"Not a whole lot," I said, smiling. "With school and all."

"What are you going to school for?"

I told him and we started talking about the classes I was currently taking.

"What about you?" I asked.

"I'll tell you if you dance with me," he said.

I took another drink of the Coke. "I don't know. I'm really not much of a dancer."

"Either am I. We'll look goofy together."

"I doubt you'd look as goofy as me," I said, finishing the rest of my soda. Besides, he looked pretty comfortable dancing with Tiffany earlier.

He stood up. "Come on, let's dance. You might feel better."

"What about Monica?" I said, looking toward the bathrooms.

"She'll figure it out."

Before I could protest any more, he grabbed my hand and pulled me toward the dance floor.

"There they are!" he hollered, pointing toward Krystal and the others.

We made our way over to where they were dancing and Krystal squealed when she saw us.

"I can't believe it. You're dancing!" she hollered, as the music changed and Jennifer Lopez's song, "On the Floor" began to play.

"I love this one!" yelled Gary, who was sweating and dancing next to two girls, who looked annoyed more than anything.

"Me, too!" cried Krystal.

"I need a drink," said Brian, pulling Krystal away from me. "You should get one, too. Cool off!"

"But I want to dance with Adriana," she protested.

"Fine. Let's have a quick drink and come back out, Birthday Girl!" he hollered over the music. "If you don't keep drinking, you're going to get sober. You don't want that, do you?"

She laughed. "When you put it that way..."

"Exactly."

"You okay, Adriana?" asked Krystal, moving toward me.

I nodded. "Just a little warm." It wasn't helping that I was now on the dancefloor with dozens of other people.

"Where's Monica?" she asked, leaning in to me.

"Bathroom," I said, feeling lightheaded. "Where's Tiffany?"

Krystal pointed and I saw that Tiffany was dancing with a guy that looked familiar.

"Isn't that one of her ex-boyfriends?" I asked.

"Yup. Oh," said Krystal as Brian grabbed her arm again and hauled her away. She laughed. "I guess I'll see you soon!"

"You okay?" asked Jason, who was now staring at my face with concern.

Suddenly it was hard to focus and the room began to spin. "Oh, wow. I'm so dizzy. We should go back, too."

"Nonsense," he said, grabbing me by the waist. "I'll take care of you."

"You know... I... I don't... feel so good," I said, my tongue thick.

"You mentioned that your drink was really strong," he said. "It must be hitting you now."

"But, I didn't drink… much," I slurred, staring up into his eyes. "This is… weird."

"You're going to be fine. I'll take care of you," he said, holding me close.

I clung on to him, afraid that I was going to fall or possibly even pass out. "I… please…I need…"

"I know what you need," he whispered in my ear before everything went black.

Chapter Six

Adriana

I woke up to find Jason helping me into the backseat of someone's car.

"What's going on?" I mumbled, trying to focus.

"I'm giving you a ride home," he said, smiling at me. "You can lie down if you want."

I tired looking outside, but it made me dizzier. "I don't remember leaving the club."

"I walked you outside to get some fresh air. You were barely coherent." He said something else, but I nodded off.

When the door slammed shut, I opened my eyes again and watched him walk around to the driver's side door. He got in and started the car.

"Where's Krystal?" I asked, feeling sick to my stomach. I rolled down the window to let some fresh air in.

"She's fine. She wanted me to take you home. You do want to go home, right? I mean, I can take you back inside if you'd prefer."

Bile rose to the back of my throat and I swallowed it down. I felt horrible and still so dizzy. I closed my eyes and curled up on the seat. "No. I just want to go home," I said, laying my head down. "Thanks, Jason. You're... so... sweet to do this..."

"You're welcome."

***

The next time I woke up, I was sitting up and Jason was in the backseat with me. One of his hands was under my sweater, the other one was trying to get inside of my jeans.

"Hey," I slurred, pushing him away. "What are you doing?"

"Shh..." he said, trying to kiss me. "Relax. I'm going to make you feel really good."

I put my hand on his chest, stopping him. "Don't."

Ignoring me, he grabbed my hand and put it on his bulging zipper. "Come on, baby, I'm so hard for you," he said. "Feel that?"

I removed my hand and shoved him firmly in the chest. "What the fuck are you doing? You asshole!"

He stiffened up. "What in the hell is your problem?"

"Me? You're acting like some kind of... rapist!" I yelled.

His face turned white and this time he backed far away from me. "No, I'm not. You were the one who was all over me! Now you're freaking out? What, are you, some kind of a psycho?"

"No," I said, trying to think back. Everything was hazy. The last thing I remembered was him promising to bring me home. "You're lying."

Jason glared at me. "I'm lying? You're completely nuts! I was going to drive you home and you had your hands all over me. Said you wanted me to come back there and fuck the shit out of you. So I pulled over. Now, you're accusing *me* of rape? What is wrong with you?"

I touched my forehead. My head was pounding and I was confused. *Fuck the shit out of me?* That certainly didn't sound like something I'd say. But to be honest, I really couldn't remember anything. "No," I said, frightened. "You have to be making this up."

He laughed coldly. "I see how it is. You're just a cock-tease. Coming on to me and then crying 'rape'. Fuck this."

Thoroughly baffled, I tried to think back, but I couldn't even remember leaving the club. But, I had. *Had* I also come on to him?

"Please, just take me home?" I asked, trying not to cry.

"Why should I take you home? I'm a rapist, remember?" he said sharply.

"Look, I'm sorry," I said, not knowing what to think anymore. "I just want to go home."

He sighed. "After the way you've treated me? You think I should just drive you home now?" He crossed his arms over his chest. "Honestly, I feel like I'm the one who's been raped."

I felt so nauseous and wondered what the hell was wrong with me. "I said I was sorry," I said, trying not to throw up. "Please, just drive me back to the club, if it's closer. I'll find Krystal or Tiffany. They'll take me home and you'll never have to see me again."

Jason's face relaxed. "I can do that, if you prefer. But," he leaned toward me and brushed a strand of hair away from my cheek, "I think you should try being a little nicer to me."

"Yeah. Sure," I said, desperately trying not to be sick. "Whatever you want. If you'll just drive me back."

"Whatever I want?"

I didn't say anything, I was too busy fighting the urge to puke.

He cupped my chin and dragged his thumb across my lower lip. "I think you know what I want," he whispered.

I could hear him unzipping his jeans and my stomach rolled. Instead of getting the blow job he obviously wanted, I leaned over and threw up all over his lap.

***

"You asshole!" I cried as Jason threw my purse out the window and it landed in the gravel. I picked it up and glared at him.

"Have fun walking," he shouted before speeding way.

Trembling, I looked around the empty parking lot, trying to figure out where I was. From what I could tell, I was at some kind of rest-stop. Unfortunately, it was dark and there wasn't anyone around.

I opened up my purse, grabbed a couple of tissues, and wiped my mouth. The jerk had gotten so pissed off at me for puking on him that he'd pushed me out of the car, totally abandoning me. Fortunately, most of the vomit had landed on him and all I was left with was the horrible taste in my mouth.

When I was done wiping my face, I walked over to a garbage can and threw the tissues away. Then I pulled out my cell phone and dialed Krystal. When she didn't answer, I left her a voicemail and then a text. Next, I called Tiffany, but she didn't answer either.

"Dammit," I mumbled, noticing that the battery on my phone was nearly dead, and it was almost two in the morning. As I considered who to call next, at such a crappy hour, I saw Raptor's number.

Fuck it, I thought. He was the one who told me to call if I had problems. This would definitely qualify. Sighing, I pressed the call button.

Chapter Seven

RAPTOR

"Get the fuck out of here," I ordered, shoving Brandy away from me. I'd found her waiting for me on my porch after leaving Griffin's. She'd been sitting there, alone in the dark, just like always. Needing me to get her off before returning to her boss.

Always loving a challenge, she ignored my anger. "Come on, baby, don't be like that," she pouted, snuggling up against me. She reached down, below my button and began caressing my cock through the fabric. "See, he already wants to come out and play."

"You've got a lot of fucking nerve," I muttered, letting her stroke me. The truth was I was still hornier than a mother-fucker and needed to do something about it. I didn't care for the whores at Griffin's and with everything that had gone on at the club, there hadn't been time to go looking for a woman who would take my mind off of Adriana's tight little ass.

"I'm sorry," whispered Brandy, rubbing her tits against my chest. She was dressed in a skirt that barely covered her crotch and a tank top that displayed her fake breasts, the ones that I'd reluctantly paid for last summer. She'd hated her B-cups, said that they didn't make her feel up to par with some of the other Old Ladies. Hell, I missed the old *Brandy*. The one before the fake boobs and even faker smiles. The one who'd promised to follow me to the moon and back.

"You're lucky I don't fucking kick your ass off of my porch," I replied in a husky voice. I looked around the neighborhood and noticed the other houses were dark. Most of my neighbors were in their twenties and thirties. Apparently, everyone was asleep or busy fucking each other. The thought made me even harder.

"I know. I can't help it, though. I need to feel you inside of me, Raptor. I miss you so much."

Should have thought of that before you fucked me over, I thought. "You miss me, huh? Tell me what you miss."

Brandy unbuckled my jeans and reached inside. "This," she whispered, pulling out my cock, which was as hard as a rock. "Oh, my God, I miss this so much."

Looking up and down the street again, I pulled her further into the shadows of my porch. "Get on your knees," I ordered.

Brandy didn't even hesitate. She got down and began sucking me off. As I watched her head bobbing and her lips sliding back and forth, I grabbed the railing behind me and closed my eyes. Instead of the lying bitch who was now getting me off, the one who'd cut me to the core with her cheating, I imagined the kitten with the green eyes and sexy smile. Adriana. Her tongue, circling the head of my cock, while she cupped my balls. Her hot, wet mouth, urging me on so she could suck me dry. It didn't take long before my hips were bucking and I was shooting my load into her mouth. Adriana's mouth.

"That was fast," said Brandy, wiping her lips.

I opened my eyes and sighed. Not fast enough as far as I was concerned. I took off my T-shirt and wiped my dick off.

"Mm… I love your muscles," she said, running her hand over my chest.

I didn't say anything, I just stared at her, unable to believe I'd wasted two years with someone like her.

"My turn, right?" she whispered, giggling nervously. "On the porch?"

I smiled coldly. "Oh, I see. You want me to munch your box on my porch?

Brandy leaned against the railing and spread her legs apart. Then she raised her skirt, exposing her hot-pink panties. The ones I'd purchased for her at Victoria's Secret. "Yeah. Mm… I'm already wet just thinking about your tongue."

Grunting, I zipped up my jeans, bundled up the T-shirt, and walked toward the front door.

"Raptor?" she pouted.

I looked over my shoulder. "Don't come back here again, Brandy."

"What the fuck? I just gave you a fucking blow job and you're going to leave me here like this? I need to get off, too, Trevor," she whined, calling me by my real name.

"Get off?" I opened the door and walked inside. Then I turned to look back at her. "Why don't you *get off* my damn porch and go home."

Her face darkened. "That's not funny."

"Not trying to be," I said. "Get out of my life and stay the fuck out this time."

She crossed her arms under her chest and smirked. "You're just saying that. I know you."

She had me there. Last week I'd been so drunk, I'd even broken down and fucked her. But, I'd had enough. "Just like I thought I knew you. You made your bed, Brandy. It's time to lay in it."

She dropped her hands and took a step toward me. "But, I want to lay in *your* bed," she pouted. "Come on, baby."

I raised my hand. "Sorry, but I don't allow whores in my bed. Not anymore. Thanks for the blow job, by the way. I've got a twenty in my wallet if you're charging for it now."

She glared at me. "You asshole."

"I prefer 'dick' but you can call me whatever you want. Just don't... call me baby," I said, before shutting the door in her face.

"Fuck you!" she hollered from the other side.

Smiling to myself, I went upstairs and took a shower.

***

Thirty minutes later, I was unwrapping a frozen pizza when my cell phone rang. Not recognizing the number, I answered it anyway.

"Raptor?"

My eyes widened. "Adriana? Is that you?"

"Uh, yeah. Listen, I need a ride home." She sighed. "You know what, I'm sorry to bother you. I should just call a cab."

"No. Wait," I said, putting the pizza back in the freezer. "I'll give you a ride. It's not a problem. Where are you?"

"I'm really not sure. Hold on."

"You at one of the clubs?"

"No," she laughed humorlessly. "Actually I'm at some rest-stop. There's a sign over here. Hold on."

"What do you mean you're at a rest-stop? Is Krystal with you?"

"No."

"Where is she?"

"I don't know," she said and then it sounded like she was crying. "Some guy brought me here. He said that he was going to take me home."

My gut clenched angrily. "What?"

"Yeah. He, um," she sniffed, "he tried making a move on me and I threw up on him."

I relaxed. "You did?"

She laughed nervously. "I don't even know what really happened or why I threw up. I mean, I hardly drank anything all night. Then I guess I passed out. When I woke up, he had his hands all over me."

"Where is this fucker?" I growled, wanting to kill the bastard. It sounded like Adriana had been slipped some kind of a date-rape drug. "The guy who did this to you?"

"Jason? I don't know. He left. Okay, I'm at Pinefield Rest Area. Do you know where that is?"

"No," I said, trying to calm down. "But, I'll find it. I'm leaving right now."

"Thanks, Raptor," she said softly.

"Call me Trevor," I said, surprised at myself.

"Thanks, Trevor."

"Watch for me. I'll get there as soon as possible."

"Okay."

Chapter Eight

Adriana

I hung up and went to the restroom facility to try and clean myself up a little, but it was locked.

"Nice," I mumbled, slinging my purse over my shoulder. I walked around the building to a picnic table and sat down. Then I took out a compact mirror and cringed at my reflection. My makeup was smeared and my eyes were red-rimmed from crying. Sighing, I tried to rub as much of the dark makeup off of my face before Trevor arrived and saw how awful I looked.

Trevor.

Although his street name Raptor was cool, I really liked his real name, Trevor. Plus, he seemed like a decent enough guy. When I'd told him about Jason, he sounded like he wanted to throttle the guy. It actually made me feel good. That and the fact that he was willing to drive out here to pick me up at such a ridiculous hour. I just hoped it wasn't for sex. I wasn't sure what I'd do if he took me back to his place and demanded I put out, to repay him. Like Jason. It was obvious Jason had wanted me to give him a blow-job. The idea started my stomach rolling all over again. Pushing away any more thoughts of that asshole, I shoved my mirror back into my purse and zipped it back up. Then I laid my head down on my arms. Fortunately, the fresh air and throwing up all over Jason had made my tummy feel better, but I was still so tired. So tired that I eventually nodded off again.

I woke up hearing the sound of a motorcycle in the distance. Wiping the drool from my lips, I grabbed my purse, hurried over to the parking lot, and stood under a light. When I saw Trevor driving toward me on his Harley, I felt such a sense of relief that I almost started crying again.

He stopped next to me and put his kickstand down, leaving the bike running. As he got off, I noticed that he wore only faded blue jeans and a black leather jacket without a shirt. His long hair was loose and windblown. In fact, he almost looked like he'd just gotten out of bed, but, truthfully, I'd never seen anyone look so good. At that moment, he was my knight-in-shining-armor and my stomach was all butterflies.

"You okay, darlin'?" he asked, studying my face.

I tried keeping a stiff upper lip, but it was hard. My emotions were all over the place. I was jittery, scared of what had happened with Jason, and yet so happy to see Trevor, that my legs felt like they were going to give out. "Yeah. I'm better. Now that you're here and can give me a lift."

He looked around and then back at me. "He just dumped you off here? In the middle of nowhere?"

I nodded and then felt my lip quivering.

Trevor's eyes softened. He opened up his arms and stepped toward me. "It's okay, Adriana. You're safe, now."

"Thanks," I squeaked, as his arms wrapped around me. I closed my eyes, surprised at how much comfort a stranger could offer. But, he was big and strong and I could tell by the look in his eyes that his concern was genuine. It made me trust him that much more.

After a few seconds, he released me and then walked back over to his bike. He opened up one of the saddlebags and pulled out another leather jacket.

"Here," he said, holding it out. "It's chilly out here. You're going to need it for the ride."

"Thanks," I replied, grabbing the black jacket. I put it on and zipped it up. "Is this yours?"

He smiled. "Yeah."

"It's nice," I said, running my hand over the soft leather. It looked expensive and new, almost like it had never been worn before. It also didn't look like something a biker would wear. It was much more… formal.

"My grandmother bought it for me a couple years ago for Christmas. She said I needed to have something classier to wear when I went out on dates," he said and then chuckled.

"Well, she has very good taste."

"She does." His smiled turned grim. "She's also one of the few people I know in my family who actually gives a shit."

"Oh. I'm sorry to hear that."

"It's okay. I wasn't asking for sympathy. I guess I was thinking out loud, again. I do that a lot."

"No problem. I do that, too."

He pushed his hair behind his ears. "So, where do you live, darlin'?"

I bit my lower lip, thinking about how loud his Harley was. It would more than likely wake up every one of the blue-hairs in the neighborhood, and there were plenty. My mom would never let me hear the end of it. Plus, she didn't like bikers. They scared her. Going home suddenly didn't seem like such a great idea.

"To tell you the truth, I don't know if I should go home right now," I said. "It's late and my mom will wake up. I don't want to have to explain…"

He looked surprised. "You live with your mom?"

I raised my chin. "Yeah. I'm in college. It's easier and more affordable."

He chuckled. "You don't have to explain anything to me, Kitten. I'm not judging you. College is expensive."

I relaxed. "You can say that again. So, um, maybe you could drive me back to Krystal's?"

"That's probably not going to work. I just spoke to Tank. Krystal's at his house."

I sighed. "Really?"

"Yep. She got a lift back to his place from some girl named Tiffany. Tank said Krystal had been under the impression that you were getting a ride home. I'm pretty sure she's passed out now with all of the shit she had to drink."

"It was supposed to have been me who was going to give her a ride home. But," I frowned, "I got sick and Jason was supposed to take me home."

Trevor's eyes hardened. "Obviously, that wasn't the fucker's only intent."

"Apparently not. I guess I can't go back Krystal's house then."

"No sweat. You can stay at my place," he said. "In the guestroom, of course," he said, when I gave him a doubtful look.

"Are you sure?" I answered, not knowing if that was a good idea. But, he did say "guest" room.

"Of course I'm sure," he said. He got on his bike and kicked up the kickstand. "Let's go."

I walked over and stood next to him, feeling nervous.

"Hop on," he said, nodding toward the seat behind him.

"To be honest, I've never been on one of these before."

"Don't worry, you're going to love it."

I smiled weakly. "Okay."

"Just get on behind me. Wait a second," he said, pointing to my purse. "Put this around your neck and shoulder. Then zip up the jacket."

I did what he said and then slid my leg over the seat, straddling the bike.

"Put your feet there," he said, pointing down to the footrests.

"Okay. How's your foot, by the way?"

"It's a little tender, but nothing to worry about."

"Good."

"I almost forgot, put this on," he said, handing me a black helmet. "Just in case."

I slipped it on and buckled it.

He grabbed one of my hands and put it around his waist. "Hold onto me tightly now. With both hands. I don't want to lose you."

"Yeah, well, I don't want you to lose me, either," I replied dryly, putting both hands around him.

"If it's more comfortable, you can slide your hands under my jacket. You might get a better grip."

"Okay," I replied, not seeing why it would make that much of a difference.

When my hands touched his bare skin, he stiffened up. "Damn, you've got cold hands, Kitten."

"Sorry," I said, enjoying how warm his skin was, not to mention how sexy his abs felt under my palms. I scooted forward until we were as close as could be and then laid my cheek against the back of his leather jacket.

He patted my knee. "Let's get you home."

Chapter Nine

RAPTOR

When Adriana's hands touched my waist, it started a fire in my lower belly and made my zipper unbearably tight. I kept my cool, however. The last thing I needed was for her to realize that I wanted to bang the fuck out of her myself, after she'd almost been raped.

"Damn, you've got cold hands, Kitten," I said, gritting my teeth as her fingers slid over my skin.

"Sorry," she said, snuggling up against me.

Releasing my breath, I patted her leg in reassurance. I wanted her to know that she was safe with me. I wasn't like that fuck-head, Jason. The one who was going to get his ass handed to him when I found the prick. "Let's get you home."

"Okay," she said, gripping my waist even more tightly as we began to roll.

I pulled out of the parking lot, relishing the fact that the roads were empty and I had a beautiful woman on the back of my bike. The only thing that could make it better would be the feel of her hand sliding further south. I brushed the lewd thoughts away and tilted my face up toward the wind, hoping it would cool me the fuck down. Here, I'd just gotten my dick sucked an hour ago and my mind was still in the gutter. But, there was something so fresh and sexy about Adriana. Something that intrigued me so much that I was out rescuing her ass at two-thirty in the morning. This was surprising, even for me. Especially after my experience with Brandy.

"You okay?" I hollered over the rumble of the engine as we turned onto the highway and began to pick up speed.

Laughing, she raised her thumb.

I smiled.

The roads were clear on the trip back to my house, but I stayed the speed limit, even taking a longer route, just so the trip would last longer. Having her on the back of my bike and holding onto me like she was felt pretty fucking good.

"I want one," said Adriana, when I pulled up to my garage, fifteen minutes later.

I smiled at her over my shoulder. "A motorcycle?"

"Yes. Oh, my God, that was *so* amazing. I can't believe I've never been on one of these before."

I turned off the engine. "It's even more amazing during the day. Especially when you're touring across the countryside with the sun in your face, your back against the wind, and the stereo cranked. It doesn't get much better than that."

"It sounds like a lot of fun. Do you take many road-trips?"

I ran my hands through my hair, wishing I would have worn it back in a ponytail. "Not enough."

"Huh." She looked around my garage. "Wow, is that your Chevelle?"

"Yeah. You into muscle cars?"

"I always thought they were cool. What year is it?"

"It's a '67 S.S."

"It's sexy," she said, walking over to it.

"I just had it repainted," I said, following her.

"What color was it before?"

"It was the same color. Black."

She leaned down and looked into the window. "It's beautiful. Do you take it out much?"

"Sometimes. It's fall now, though, so I probably won't take it out any more this year," I replied.

"I don't blame you," she said turning around. When she noticed how close we were, she slid sideways and moved around me. "Thanks for letting me stay at your place. The fresh air felt great, but I'm so tired. I can't wait to sleep."

"I bet. Do you have to work later?" I asked, not even sure if she had a job. All I knew was that she was in college.

She nodded. "Yeah. At six-thirty. In the evening, thank God."

"Where do you work?"

"I work part-time at Dazzle."

"The jewelry store?"

Adriana nodded. "My mom owns it. Normally I don't work Saturday nights, but I promised I'd help her with inventory after the shop closes"

"Huh. I've been there, before. Nice stuff. A little pricey, but nice."

"You pay for quality," she replied. "My mother prides herself on buying only the best diamonds and gems. She travels all over for them."

"Interesting. Does she make her own jewelry, too?"

"Yes. She's been teaching me now, too."

"Really? That must be interesting."

She shrugged. "It's okay. I don't have the same passion that she does. Or creativity. Anyway, what about you? Where do you work?"

"You mean when I'm not working for Slammer?"

"Yeah."

"I do a little carpentry on the side."

She looked surprised. "Like, as in fixing up houses and stuff?"

"Yeah," I said, as we stepped outside the garage and began heading toward the house. "Or whatever else needs fixing."

She stopped abruptly. "Um, it looks like you have company and… they might need some fixing of their own."

I looked to see what she was staring at and my blood began to boil. Brandy was standing on my porch, holding a tissue and glaring at us.

"What are you doing here?" I asked sharply.

Her face fell and she began to cry.

"Fuck," I mumbled when I noticed the bruise on her cheek.

"Danny hit me," she said, raising her chin. "If you didn't notice."

I stepped onto the porch. "Yeah, well, what the fuck do you want me to do about it?"

Adriana, who was behind me, gasped at my indifference.

Brandy looked at her. "Who the hell is this?"

"Never mind," I snapped. "It's none of your business. Now, get in your car and go home."

"Trevor, I *can't* go home," she cried, looking at me like I was an idiot. "He kicked me out. I need a fucking place to stay."

Grinding my teeth, I unlocked the front door and turned to Adriana. "I have some shit to take care of," I said, trying to soften my voice. "Go inside and make yourself at home."

"Uh, I can call a cab," she said, looking a little uncomfortable.

I gave her a reassuring smile. "No cab. Everything is cool, okay? I'll be in shortly."

She nodded.

"Oh, and hey… if you'd like to take a shower, there are towels in the linen closet. Feel free to use whatever you want."

Brandy wrinkled her nose and smirked. "She should. She smells like puke."

I turned to her. "Brandy," I warned, glaring at her. "Shut the fuck up."

"I'll be inside," said Adriana, walking past me. From the look on her face, she was as embarrassed as all hell.

"Who the fuck is she *really*, Trevor?" said Brandy, after Adriana shut the door.

"Like I said, it's none of your goddamn business," I said and pointed toward the street where her car was parked. "Now, take your problems somewhere else. They don't belong here."

Her lip quivered and her eyes filled with tears. "Why are you such an asshole? Don't you care about me at all?"

I stared at her in disbelief. "I stopped caring the moment I found out you were fucking around on me with your boss, who I assume is now your *EX* boss. You're lucky I didn't beat the fuck out of you when I found out, because you'd have had more than a bruise on your cheek."

She tilted her head and smiled. "Right. That's not you."

"Maybe it should be," I threatened, never wanting to hit a woman as much as I did at that moment.

She saw through it. "You're a good man, Trevor. You'd never hit a woman. We both know that."

I smiled cruelly. "Is that right? Just like I thought I knew you?"

Brandy's face fell. She tried reaching for me. "Trevor, baby, I'm so sorry –"

I pushed her away. "Don't you give me that 'I'm sorry' shit and don't you dare fucking test me," I spat. "Now, if you don't get off of my property, I'll call the police and let them do it."

Her eyes widened. "*You* call the police. That's hilarious."

"Does it look like I'm doing stand-up now?" I whispered angrily, noticing that one of my neighbors' porches was now lit up.

Brandy let out a ragged sigh. "Okay, fine. But, do you even care why he hit me?"

"Nope."

She ignored me. "I told him I wanted to get back with you."

Grunting, I opened the door. "That's priceless."

She lurched forward, grabbing onto my leather jacket. "Please, Trevor, forgive me," she begged, staring up into my eyes. "I made a mistake, baby. I realize that. It was the biggest mistake of my life, but I know that somehow… we can both get past it."

I removed her hands from my collar and shoved her away. "It's too late, Brandy, don't you get it?"

"But I made a mistake," she sobbed. "I should have never cheated on you. I know that. Can't you just forgive me?"

I hated seeing a woman cry, especially one I'd once cared so much about. But my pride was still wounded and there was no way I'd be able to ever trust Brandy again. Not after the shit she'd pulled. "Seems to me you didn't learn your lesson after balling your boss."

She looked confused. "What do you mean?"

"You cheated on me and then you cheated on Danny, *with* me. Well, guess what? Now, neither of us want anything to do with your lying ass," I said, slamming the door in her face.

Chapter Ten

Adriana

I wasn't exactly sure who the blond was standing on Trevor's porch but she certainly didn't look thrilled to see me. And the comment about me smelling like puke – well, it was probably true, but she didn't have to point it out. Beaten or not, she was still a bitch.

Sighing, I turned on the light, removed my boots, and caught my first impression of Trevor's place. From what I could tell, it was a cozy, split-level house that couldn't have been more than ten years old. It smelled kind of nice, too. Like fresh cedar and lemon. It was a nice surprise, considering I'd expected it to smell more like cigarettes or stale beer, since he was a biker and obviously liked to party.

To the left of the front door, I noticed a pair of Nike tennis shoes, a brown pair of cowboy boots, and a set of steel-toed mountain boots sitting next to a wooden bench. I placed my own boots next to his.

Damn, he has big feet.

Smiling, I walked up the stairs, to the main level, which was obviously a bachelor pad. There was an oversized brown leather sectional, which faced a large television and an impressive stereo and sound system. There was also a large fish tank that took up most of the other wall. Other than that, there wasn't much thought put into the decor, save for a few candles and a painting of an older model Harley Davidson, which hung over a small fireplace.

Intrigued by the aquarium, I walked over and stared at the colorful fish, which were obviously the saltwater kind. I leaned down and watched a group of clown-fish swim through some rocks, amazed at the sheer size of the tank. I didn't know a lot about fish, but I knew that a large tank like this wasn't cheap and needed a lot of maintenance. As I began examining some of the other fish, the front door opened and then seconds later, slammed shut, startling me. I straightened up and met him by the stairs. He looked like he wanted to hurt someone.

"So, is she going to be all right?" I asked, nodding toward the doorway.

He grunted and shook his head. "She was a total cunt to you and yet you still care about her welfare?"

I winced at the word "cunt." I hated it, but for some reason, it seemed kind of fitting for her. "I don't know. She just looked so desperate. Like she really needed help."

"Don't worry about her. She'll be fine. She can go to her sister's or her mom's for help," he said, climbing the steps.

"Who is she?" I asked, having a pretty good idea.

"She's... nobody."

"*Nobody*, who visits you in the middle of the night?" I replied.

He sighed and removed his leather jacket. "She used to be my Old Lady. Before she decided she needed to be more than that."

I stared at his bare chest and muscular arms, wondering why in the hell she'd given all that up. "Her loss though, right?"

Trevor smiled. "That's what I keep telling myself," he said, walking closer to me.

I grinned.

"How are you feeling? Still sick to your stomach?"

I shrugged. "A little. I think I just need to sleep."

He nodded.

"So, you said I could use your shower?" I asked, feeling nervous now that we were alone in his house and he was already half-naked.

"Oh, yeah," he said, turning toward the hallway. "There's a shower you can use right through here. I'll show you."

"Okay."

I followed him to the bathroom and he turned on the light.

"Everything you need should be in there – shampoo, conditioner, soap…"

"Thanks," I said, as he reached inside the linen closet and handed me a thick, blue towel.

He looked down at my clothes. "Oh, yeah. You'll probably need something clean to wear. I'll be right back," he said, leaving me in the bathroom. He returned shortly with a pair of red boxers and a long black Harley Davidson T-shirt. "I don't know if these will fit," he said, nodding toward the boxers, "but the T-shirt should be comfortable enough."

"Thanks," I replied, taking them from him. I smiled shyly. "You've been so nice. I don't even know what to say."

"Don't worry about it. I'm just glad I could help."

"Me, too," I said, trying not to stare at his biceps. But it was hard. Not only were they nice but his tattoos were intriguing. "What is that on your upper arm? The face with the empty eyes?"

He looked down at it. "I got that when I was sixteen. It's supposed to represent a soulless asshole."

"Your father?"

He chuckled. "No. Me. Back then. I was going through some things. I had a lot of anger issues. Got into a lot of fights. Did some shit I wasn't proud of."

"We all did."

His eyes twinkled. "You like to make up excuses for people. You need to stop doing that."

I couldn't help but smile. "You think so?"

"Definitely. You're far too nice."

"I'll work on it."

He smirked. "You have any ink?"

"Tattoos? Me?" I laughed. "No. Not that I don't want one. Maybe someday."

"You could start out with something small. Like a heart. Then build from there."

"I was thinking a skull would be kind of cool. A skull with a rose."

He grinned. "You like skulls?"

"I like flowers. I just thought the skull would make it look not so… girly."

"Nothing wrong with being girly," he said. "But, having a dark side can also be damn sexy. You have one of those?"

"A dark side?"

He gave me a slow grin. "Yeah."

My cheeks turned pink. "Maybe. Maybe not."

"I don't think you do," he replied. "But, to tell you the truth, it doesn't make you any less sexy."

I could feel my blush deepen.

He suddenly looked like he'd gotten his hand caught in the cookie jar. "Sorry. I'd better let you get into the shower so you can get some rest."

"Thanks. Where is the guestroom?"

"It's right next to my bedroom," he said. "Down the hall and to the left. There should be clean sheets on it and the mattress is decent. It's not as nice as mine, though. So, if you want, I can take the guest bed and you can have my room."

"No. I'm sure the bed is just fine. Thanks, though."

Nodding, he shoved his hands into his pockets. "If you change your mind and have a hard time sleeping, you can always sneak into my bed. It's a king and I pretty much sleep like the dead. I doubt I'd even know you were there."

I laughed. "Right. I bet you say that to all your female guests."

He looked serious. "I know what you've been through tonight. There's no way I'd take advantage of you, Adriana. I'm serious."

I smiled. "I appreciate it. I'll be fine though. In the guestroom."

He nodded. "Okay. Well, I'm going to make a phone call, so when you're done with your shower, feel free to crash. Unless you're hungry, that is. Would you like something to eat? I was about to make a pizza before I left to pick you up."

My stomach was empty but food just didn't sound that appetizing. "No, thanks. I'm just going to go to bed."

"Okay. Holler if you need anything," he said, leaving me alone in the bathroom.

"Thanks," I replied, shutting the door.

I turned around and looked at myself in the mirror. Sure enough, there was dried puke in my hair. Not a lot, but enough to be offensive.

He had to have seen it.

I was too tired to even care. Sighing, I turned on the water, got undressed, and slipped into the shower.

Chapter Eleven

RAPTOR

After leaving Adriana, I walked into my bedroom, changed into a pair of sweats, and called Tank back.

"She okay?" he mumbled, answering the phone.

"Yeah. Sorry, brother. Did I wake you?"

"It's okay. What happened?"

I told him what I knew.

"Fucker must have slipped something into her drink."

"That's what I was thinking," I said. "What about Krystal? You think anything made it into hers?"

"No. She was definitely drunk, but coherent. Rode me like I was a goddamn bull. I swear, my balls are sore from all that bouncing around."

I chuckled.

"I'm serious. The woman was insatiable tonight."

"Okay, enough about your horny woman and your hairy balls. You're making me sick."

He laughed. "So, what do you want to do about this guy?"

"Teach him a fucking lesson."

"That's what I thought. We'll start looking tonight. Obviously, he didn't get laid. He'll be sure as shit looking for someone else to molest on a Saturday night."

"I'm counting on it."

"What the fuck is it about this date-rape shit? Why can't they just be fucking men and earn the pussy? It's more fun that way anyway."

I stretched out on my bed and stared up at the ceiling. "It's not about the sex. I heard it's about controlling the victim."

"Okay, Dr. Phil."

"Fuck off. It's what I heard."

He chuckled. "I'm just giving you shit. I actually heard that, too. On Oprah."

I laughed. "You still watch that show, huh?"

"How do you think Dr. Phil got started? Oprah's a fucking genius. Everything she touches turns to gold."

"If your old man knew you were watching Oprah," I said, chuckling, "he'd kick your ass."

"Fucking tell him and I'll kick yours."

"Doesn't Oprah condemn violence?"

"For you, I'm sure she'd make an exception. Anyway, back to this fucking dirt-bag. You know, he probably won't hit the same club."

"Probably not. We'll get a description and spread out. I'm sure Hopper, Derby, and Jackal wouldn't mind helping out. We can do it before the card game tomorrow."

"Agreed. Hell, I think we should round up our *entire* posse and catch ourselves a rabbit. Feed him to the Raptor. Unless you want to just shoot the guy?"

The thought had entered my mind. "That's letting him down too easy."

"True."

"So, what's going on with Breaker?" I asked, changing the subject. "Is there going to be any kind of retribution for what happened to Jessica?"

"The Rangers are still standing behind that lying sack of shit."

"Fuck."

"You can say that again. The old man is spitting bullets. I'm thinking he's just going to say 'fuck it' and take him out anyway." He lowered his voice. "Don't say anything, but I guess she was a virgin to boot."

I groaned.

"What a way to have your cherry popped, huh?"

"No shit," I said. "He beat the fuck out of her, too, didn't he?"

"From what I hear, he knocked her around, pretty good. The old man is so fucking pissed. He's not going to let this slide."

"I don't blame him. That pile of shit needs to be taken the fuck out. Even if he didn't rape Jessica, he sure as shit is going to assault someone else," I said, thinking of the way he'd been harassing Adriana earlier.

"He did it. There's no doubt in my mind, or Pop's."

"So, what now?"

"He mentioned contacting The Judge."

The Judge was a mercenary who didn't belong to any club that I knew of. He was a discreet motherfucker who always got the job done, no matter what it was. For a hefty price, though.

"He know how to get ahold of him?" I asked.

"Apparently. It's his godson."

That was a shock. "I didn't know that."

"You're not supposed to."

"Then I'll keep it to myself."

"I know you will, brother."

I ran a hand over my forehead. I was beat and couldn't wait to sleep myself. "Are we still having church tomorrow afternoon?"

"Yeah. Three o'clock."

"Okay."

"You like her, don't you."

"Who?"

Tank laughed. "What do you mean, *who*? You know who the fuck I mean. The chick. Adriana."

I hesitated. "She's okay."

"You going to tap that?"

"Fuck no. She was almost raped. I'd have to be a real asshole to even try."

"You are a real asshole," he chided, a smile in his voice.

"Fuck off."

"I'm just giving you shit. She's cute. I think she was digging you earlier."

"Doesn't matter. She's... different. I'm leaving her be."

"Different. Like how?"

"She's... a gullible suburban girl."

He tried goading me again. "Your address is in the suburbs."

"You know what the fuck I mean."

"I'm seeing Krystal. They're friends. She lives in the suburbs. I don't see the problem."

"Come on, Tank. You know what I'm talking about. These are both the kinds of girls that want commitment, a ring, and a piece of paper. They won't stand for anything less."

"I'm going to patch her and who knows... maybe someday we'll get hitched."

"Krystal? You really care that much for her?" I asked, surprised.

"Yeah, I do."

"This is fucking weird," I said, smirking. "We're on the phone and talking about relationships. We sound like a couple of fucking chicks. I'd better get off before I start growing tits and talking about shoes."

Tank laughed. "I hear you, brother. Okay. Catch you later."

"Sounds good."

I hung up the phone and was plugging it into the charger on my nightstand when I heard Adriana open the door and step out of the bathroom. I quickly got out of bed and met her in the hallway. Her hair was wrapped in a towel and her face was slightly pink.

"Feel better?" I asked.

She nodded. "What should I do with the towel?" she asked, touching her head.

"I can take it. What did you do with your clothes?"

"Oh, crap, I forgot. I left them in the bathroom," she said, moving back inside. She bent down and scooped them up.

"Give them to me and I'll wash them. That way they'll be clean when you're ready to go later."

"You don't have to go through all of that trouble," she said, stepping back out of the bathroom. "Seriously. You've already done enough."

"Don't worry about it. I'm sure you're not going to want to put them back on later dirty. Although, you do look pretty comfortable in my T-shirt," I said, my eyes trailing over her chest to her slender legs. *I should have given her a white T-shirt*, I thought. "So, uh, how do the boxers fit?"

She lifted the shirt, baring her stomach. "They're pretty baggy," she said, tugging at the waistband. "But, they'll do."

"You just don't fill them out the way I do."

She suddenly looked embarrassed. Adriana dropped the T-shirt. "I'm sure."

I cleared my throat and nodded toward the guestroom. "You may as well try and get some sleep. I'm going to throw your things into the wash machine. Did you want me to wake you at a certain time?"

"Just when you want to kick me out."

"That's the last thing I want to do," I replied, thinking out loud.

She laughed nervously. "Okay. Well, I guess by ten?"

"Sure," I said, holding out my arms. "I'll take care of the laundry and then I'm going to crash, myself."

"Thanks again," she said, handing me the clothes. She then touched my arm. "You've been so incredibly sweet to me."

I grunted. "Just don't tell anyone. You'll ruin my reputation for being a soulless asshole."

"Your secret is safe with me, Raptor," she replied before leaning over and kissing me on the cheek.

Resisting the urge to drop everything and kiss her back properly, I turned on my heel and headed toward the laundry room. "Sleep well, Kitten."

"Thanks. You, too," she called back.

Chapter Twelve

Adriana

Trevor had been right – the full-sized guest bed wasn't the most comfortable. In fact, it was as hard as a rock. I was so exhausted that it didn't matter, however. I fell asleep within two minutes of hitting the pillow.

When Trevor woke me a few hours later, my back was stiff and I had a horrible headache.

"You okay?" he asked, staring down at me, holding a cup of coffee. He was dressed in pale blue jeans, a white T-shirt, and his leather cut. His blond hair was down and slightly damp.

I sat up and winced. "Headache."

"I've got something for that. Hold on," he said, disappearing out of the room.

I swung my legs over the side of the bed and sat there, listening to him rummage around in the bathroom. He returned with two pills and a bottle of water.

"Advil."

I took them from him. "Thanks."

"No problem. Are you hungry?"

"Very," I replied, feeling my stomach growl at the mention of it.

"Good, because I'm making us breakfast."

I smiled. "That sounds great. Thank you."

He nodded toward the dark oak dresser where I noticed that my clothes were sitting. "Your clothes are clean. Get dressed and I'll meet you in the kitchen."

"Okay," I said, opening up the bottle of water. I shoved the pills into my mouth and washed them down.

He started walking out of the room and then turned back.

"What?" I asked, wondering why he was staring at me with such a funny smile.

"I was just thinking, I've had a lot of women stay overnight in this place, and I've never seen anyone look so good in the morning. Without makeup."

"Right," I said, resisting the urge to look at myself in the dresser mirror.

"No, I'm serious. You obviously have great genes. Your mother must be a gorgeous woman," he said before leaving the room.

Thinking about her, I quickly stood up. "Crap, where's my phone?" I called.

"Your purse is in the kitchen," he hollered back.

I closed the door, changed my clothes, and then glanced in the mirror. "He must be either blind or looking to get laid," I mumbled, staring at my reflection. My hair was a mess from drying overnight on the pillow, and there was still some mascara blotches under my lashes. Sighing, I ran my fingers through my hair, and then licked my finger to wipe off the black crud. When I cleaned what I could, I walked into the kitchen, where the smell of bacon made me groan in pleasure.

"It smells wonderful in here."

"Thanks."

"A man who can cook," I said, watching him flip the eggs. "Nice."

"I can hold my own. Hope you like your eggs over-easy, 'cause that's how I made them."

"That's how I like them," I said, sitting down at the table.

"You want some coffee?"

"No thanks. I'm not much of a coffee drinker," I answered and then held up the bottle of water. "I'll just drink the rest of this."

He grabbed two plates and set them on the counter. "I've got orange juice."

"The water is fine."

He glanced over his shoulder at me. "You like orange juice?"

"Yeah."

"Then you're drinking it," he said, filling the plates with food. "After last night, the vitamin C will be good for you."

"Uh, okay."

He brought the plates over and set one in front of me.

"Wow, this is a lot of food," I said, staring down at my plate. There were two eggs, a pile of hash browns, along with two pieces of toast, and four strips of bacon. "I normally have yogurt or a muffin for breakfast."

"Explains why you're so skinny."

"I'm healthy, though."

He opened the refrigerator and took out a carton of orange juice. "I'm not saying you're not. Just mentioning that you're skinny."

It was weird. I wondered if he thought I was too skinny. "Okay."

Grinning, he poured some of the orange juice into a glass and then set it down next to my plate.

"Why do you keep grinning?" I asked.

"Why are you so insecure?"

"I'm not insecure," I said defensively.

His grin widened.

"What is so damn funny?" I asked again, seeing the amusement in his eyes. "I just, I just don't get it."

He sat across from me. "Nothing, really. I just like fucking with you."

"I can tell."

Our eyes met.

"You can tell what?"

"That you like fucking with me," I said.

He got a wicked look in his eyes and I thought he was going to come back with something crude, but then his face grew serious. Clearing his throat, he grabbed the bottle of ketchup and began pouring some on his hash browns. "You do realize what happened last night, don't you?"

"I think so."

"Tell me."

I sighed. I'd thought it about it before drifting off to sleep. Nothing else made any sense other than Jason, or one of his friends, must have slipped something into my drink. Some kind of drug. I just didn't know if I could prove it. "I think that maybe someone slipped drugged me."

"That guy, Jason?"

"I'm not totally sure. I think it was him, but it could have been one of his friends. They bought us shots and drinks. I don't know, maybe I'm being silly. Maybe it was something else. Food poisoning. A touch of the flu. I don't know."

"How much did you drink?

"One shot. A couple sips of a rum and Coke."

"That's it?"

"Jason bought me a soda. I drank that and then we went out on the dance floor."

A vein in Trevor's forehead began to pulsate. He looked pissed. "He bought you the soda. That's what I wanted to hear. Do you know where to find him?"

"Not really. I mean, we both go to the same college, I.U., but the campus is huge. I'll probably never see him again."

"What kind of a car was he driving?"

"I think it was a Camry. Four-door."

"Color?"

I closed my eyes and thought back. "I think it was dark blue," I said, opening them back up.

"What about his friends? Is there anything you can tell me about them?"

My eyes widened. "Why?"

"He needs to be stopped."

I sighed. "Yeah. I suppose I should call the police. Maybe it's not too late to find out if I really was drugged."

"You were obviously drugged, probably with GHB. Anyway, we're not calling the police," he said, picking up his fork.

"Why? You just said he needed to be stopped. God, I wonder how many times he's done this before?" I said, staring at my plate of food. It didn't quite look so appetizing anymore. "GHB, huh? I've heard of that stuff. Just never thought it would happen to me."

"He'll be stopped, Kitten. Believe me. But we're not getting the police involved. It would be a waste of time."

"What exactly are you planning on doing?" I asked, feeling anxious now. Obviously, Jason was an asshole and should be arrested, but something told me that Trevor's plans for him were more sinister. And violent.

"Nothing you need to know about," he said and then nodded at my food. "Now, eat. You've got to be hungry."

I bit my lower lip. "You're going to do something illegal, aren't you?"

He didn't answer.

"Are you planning on hurting him?"

He picked up a piece of toast and dipped it into his eggs. "First of all, why do you care? And secondly, how many girls do you think he's already hurt or will hurt?"

"I don't know but we need to let the cops take care of this."

"There won't be any evidence that he did anything. It will be a waste of time."

"What do you mean? Maybe they can test my blood for proof that I was drugged."

"If it's GHB, the shit dissipates in your blood pretty quickly, from what I hear. And even if they do find something, how can you prove he actually did it? Did you see him put anything into your drink?"

"No."

"And it was a crowded bar."

"Yeah."

"It will be your word against his. No evidence."

"He might have some of the drug in his car or his home. The police can get a search warrant."

"You really want to waste your time filling out a bunch of police reports and waiting for test results, only to find out later that they don't have any real evidence to arrest the asshole?"

I let out a ragged breath. "No. I guess not. I have to work tonight and I've got classes on Monday."

"There you go. Let me handle it."

"What exactly are you planning on doing?"

He didn't say anything.

"Trevor?"

He sighed. "We'll just scare the fuck out of him. Let him know he can't get away with that shit."

I frowned. "That's really all that you're going to do?"

"Yeah. Sure. Why do you care what happens to that prick, anyway?"

"I just don't want to see anyone get hurt. "

"Jesus, you really are a bleeding-heart, aren't you?"

I pictured Trevor getting arrested and it did something to me. "I just don't want to see you get thrown in jail."

"I won't."

"You could."

"Don't worry about me."

"Why would you even risk it? For me? We barely know each other."

He took a moment to answer. "Let's just say that I despise assholes who fucking abuse women like that. Whether it's drugging them, pushing them around, or whatever the fuck they're doing." His jaw clenched. "I told you how my dad used to beat the fuck out of my mom. Had to watch that shit happen for years, until I finally had the balls to stand up to him. It may have not turned out the way I'd imagined it, but it still made me feel good. Showing my old man that I wasn't going to let him get away with that shit. Not while I was around."

"You should be proud of yourself," I said. "You were obviously a very brave kid."

"I was actually scared shitless at the time. But, I made a promise to myself that I'd never stand back and watch anyone get kicked around that didn't deserve it. Never again. Especially, women."

"So, if you wanted to make a difference in that respect, why didn't you become a cop instead of a... gang member?"

His face grew dark. "Because this has been my life since Slammer took me in. I'd do anything for any one of my brothers. We're family. They've got my back and I've got theirs."

"Yeah, but, if you're so passionate about stopping violence again women, becoming a cop –"

"Don't get me started on cops. Hell, the cops couldn't help my mom. Even the times the neighbors called them and they took my old man away. He always came back, whether it was the next day or the next week. Sure, they'd make up and everything would be good for a while. But, just for a while. Then he'd beat the shit out of her again."

I didn't know what to say. Living through that would have taken away any faith I had in the legal system, too. Not that it was directly the cops' fault. His mom had obviously allowed it to happen until she finally took off on her own.

I remained silent and he seemed to relax. "Listen to me, don't you go worrying your pretty little head about what's gonna happen to Jason. You feel me?"

I nodded. If he wanted to confront Jason, I wasn't going to stand in the way. The asshole certainly didn't deserve any pity from me. "Sure… I, uh, feel you."

"Good." He pointed at my plate with his fork. "Now, eat your food and if it makes you feel better, forget that we ever had this conversation."

"I think I will," I replied, cutting into my egg.

Chapter Thirteen

Adriana

We didn't say much more during breakfast. I could tell he had a lot on his mind and so did I. When we were finished, I offered to help him with the dishes.

"I'll do them," he said and then nodded to my purse. "You need to call someone? Let them know you're okay?"

"That's right. I was going to call my mom," I said, grabbing the phone out of my purse. I walked into the living room and dialed her number. When she didn't answer, I left her message about staying overnight at a friend's, and that I'd see her later. Just as I was hanging up, Lily called me.

"What happened last night?" she asked.

I gave her the play-by-play and she gasped.

"Jason told me you asked him to drive me home. Did you?"

"You could barely stand and I thought you were wasted. I mean, yeah, the guy offered to do it and he seemed so nice."

"Obviously it was all an act."

"I'm so sorry, Adriana. I had no fucking idea that he'd pull that kind of shit."

"Yeah, well, I'm still shocked myself."

She sighed. "Do you even remember leaving the club?"

"Not really. I can remember him helping me into the car. Then, I passed out and the next thing I knew, he had his hands all over me."

"Oh, my God, you must have been scared."

"I was confused and then pissed off, more than anything."

"I feel like such an idiot. He almost raped you," she said, her voice cracking. "I'm so sorry. I shouldn't have let him drive you home."

"It's not your fault. You were pretty tipsy yourself."

"Yeah, I was trashed. So was Tiffany. Thank God she made it home herself after dropping me off."

"What happened with Monica?"

"She went home, right after you did."

I sighed. "Do you think that Jason's friends were involved?"

"Maybe. I don't know. Gary didn't seem the type. I mean, he and I talked about his ex-girlfriend and he started crying. I can't imagine him pulling something like that. Unless it was all a fucking act."

"What about Brian?" I asked, lowering my voice.

"It's hard to say. I'm pretty sure nobody put anything into my drink. Or Tiff's." She then explained that the four of them shut down the bar and then went their separate ways.

"Brian even asked me for my phone number," she said. "I think he wanted more than that last night, and to be truthful, I probably would have if Tank wouldn't have sent me a text."

"Are you still at Tank's?"

"No, I'm on my way home. He dropped me off at my car. Anyway, are you still at Raptor's?"

"Yes."

She sucked in her breath. "Did you two fuck?"

"Oh, my God, no!" I said a little sharply. Then I lowered my voice. "It's not like I was in the mood for anything like that. Not after what happened."

"Yeah, I suppose not. Sorry."

"It's okay. I mean, yeah... he's definitely interesting," I said and then turned around to find him listening behind me. I quickly turned away. "I have to go. I'll call you later."

"Call me before nine. I'm going back out to the club again tonight. With Tank and Raptor. They want to search for that guy, Jason."

I frowned. "That's another thing. What if I wasn't really drugged?"

"You had to have been. Looking back, there's no way that you could have been that drunk after one shot and a measly rum and Coke. Something was definitely wrong."

I sighed. "Maybe."

"No *maybe*. You were slipped something. Anyway, I gotta go. I just pulled into my driveway. Talk to you later?"

"Yeah. I'll call you."

We hung up and I turned back to Trevor, who was staring at me with a stern face.

"What?" I asked.

He crossed his arms over his chest. "You *were* drugged. I don't know why you're having a hard time accepting it."

I let out a ragged sigh. "I know. It's just so… surreal, you know? It's like it happened to someone else."

"I wish it would have. Tell you one thing, it definitely happened to the wrong girl," he said. "Because now, that fucker is going to pay for what he did."

It was unsettling to see such determination on Trevor's face. Although, we'd just met the night before, he was acting like Jason had attacked him personally. Part of me was flattered that he wanted to avenge me. Another part of me was a little overwhelmed by everything.

"I suppose I should get back home," I said, noticing that it was getting close to noon.

"No problem. Let me grab some stuff and we'll head out."

"Okay."

I used the bathroom while he got ready, and then followed him back out to the garage.

"You don't mind taking the bike again, do you?"

"Not at all," I said. It was a beautiful day. It had to be almost sixty degrees, and the sun was shining.

"You want my leather coat again?" he asked, slipping on his jacket.

"I'm okay. My sweater is warm," I answered. "And you're blocking most of the wind."

"True. Feel free to warm your hands on me, if you get too cold."

"Okay."

He looked like he was about to say something else, but then seemed to change his mind.

"What?"

"Nothing," he said, his lip curling up.

I smirked. "Right. With that look on your face, I could tell it was something."

Something dirty, more than likely.

He put his sunglasses on. "You think you've gotten me all figured out?"

"Hardly."

"That's probably good. I have a feeling if you did know the real me, you'd run for the hills."

I smiled. "Maybe. But not before we take another ride on your motorcycle."

Chuckling, he got on his Harley and started it. "Ready?"

I swung my leg over the bike and we took off.

Chapter Fourteen

Raptor

Adriana told me where she lived and I took the scenic route so she could enjoy the ride and I could enjoy her arms around me that much longer.

When we arrived at her home, I was a little taken aback. Having found out that her mother owned 'Dazzle', I'd expected, I don't know… a mansion in the hills or something that hinted of wealth. Instead, her house was small and quaint, and nestled inside of a quiet little neighborhood, inhabited by retirees who apparently spent most of their days making their yards immaculate.

As I shut off my bike, the front door of her house opened and a woman stepped outside. She had a smile on her face, but the look in her eyes was frosty.

"Crap," mumbled Adriana, getting off of the bike. "I thought she'd be at work."

I could tell right away where Adriana got her beauty from. The woman had the same dark hair and green eyes that she had, although her skin was a slightly more olive, and she was much shorter.

"Hi, Mom," said Adriana, as the woman approached us

"So, this is the friend you mentioned in your message?" she asked, looking at me like I was some kind of leper.

"Uh, yes. This is Trevor. Trevor, this is my mom, Vanda."

"Nice to meet you," I said, trying to be cordial under the circumstances. The circumstances being that she didn't like me.

Vanda nodded and looked at my leather jacket. Her face went from unfriendly to downright hostile. "You're in a gang?"

"We call it a club," I said, not liking the way she said it.

Vanda looked at Adriana and said something in what I assume was Portuguese. She answered back quickly, and then they proceeded to argue about something. Something, obviously being, *me*.

"Well, I think this is my cue to leave," I said, dryly. "I'll keep in touch, Kitten."

"Uh, okay," she replied, looking embarrassed.

I turned to Vanda. "Glad we had this chance to get to know each other," I said. "Your daughter has my number, Vanda, if you'd like to give me a call sometime. We can pick up where we left off."

Vanda's eyebrows raised and she almost looked amused. But it was quickly replaced by what I could only describe as indifference. And maybe relief.

"Goodbye," she said, and then turned and walked back toward the house.

Adriana glared at her mother's back.

I sighed. "She's a tough win."

Adriana turned to look at me. She touched my arm. "I'm sorry. My mother had a bad experience with some bikers once. She's frightened of all of you now."

"I wouldn't call that frightened," I said, smiling. "Hell, she seemed like she was ready kick my ass."

"I know; she was more angry at me than anything else."

"What happened?"

She sighed. "My parents' store was robbed about ten years ago."

"By some bikers?"

"Yes. We lived in Florida at the time."

"What club?"

"Hell's Demons, I believe they were called."

"Oh. Those fucking guys. Yeah, they're assholes. The ones that I've met, anyway. Did the bastards who did it go to prison?"

"Actually, the police never caught the guys who did it. They had masks on."

"So now she doesn't trust anyone wearing patches?"

"She doesn't trust bikers, period."

I looked at the house and saw Adriana's mother staring at us from inside of the doorway.

"I guess I can't blame her, but she shouldn't lump all of us in a pot like that. I've never robbed anyone in my life. None of my brothers have, either."

"I know. Anyway, forget about her. I'm not going to let her opinion change my mind about you."

I grinned. "And what is your mind telling you about me?"

"That you're a decent guy."

"Decent. I don't know about that," I said, thinking back to some of the things I'd done in my life, especially in my teens. I may not have robbed anyone, but I had a temper. I'd lost it more times than I could count. I also had the scars on my fists to prove it.

"Well, you've been good to me," she said, kissing me on the cheek again.

As she was about to pull away, I grabbed her around the waist and pulled her to me, kissing her fully on the lips. She stiffened up but then to my delight, began kissing me back. Relaxing, I slid my hand around the back of her head and shoved my tongue inside, wanting to taste every part of her.

"We can't," she said, pulling away, suddenly.

I frowned. "Says who?"

She looked over her shoulder at the house. "My mom's watching us."

"So. Let her watch," I said, trying to pull her back to me.

"You don't understand. She's going to freak out."

As if on cue, the front door opened and Vanda stuck her head out. "Adriana!" she hollered, looking furious. "I need you! Come inside."

"I'll be right there!" she yelled back.

Vanda said something in her language.

Adriana rolled her eyes, but didn't answer back.

"You want a kiss goodbye, too?" I called out. "All you have to do is ask."

Vanda glared at me and closed the door.

I smiled grimly. "Fucking-A. How old are you, Kitten?"

"I know," she said, her face flushed. "Believe it or not, she's normally not like this."

"I want to see you again," I said, starting up my bike. "And from the way you were kissing me back, you feel the same."

"I don't think it's a good idea."

"Why not?"

She nodded toward the house.

***

Adriana

Trevor's eyes burned into mine. They were filled with lust and anger. Before I could react, he grabbed my wrist and pulled me back over to him, taking my mouth, hard and fast. Then, just as quickly, he released me.

"You're a grown woman. You can do what you want, see who you want, and fuck who you want," he said, his eyes burning with frustrated need. "And something tells me that right now, we both want the same thing."

I found myself panting, he had me so worked up. Had we been alone, there was no doubt in my mind that we'd be all over each other until I made sure that he was inside of me, putting out the fire he'd started. The guy definitely knew how to kiss a woman.

"Adriana!" called my mother again.

I jerked my head toward her. She was definitely treating me like a child. It made me so angry and embarrassed that I almost jumped back on his bike, just to spite her.

"You'd better go and see what she wants," said Trevor, smirking. "Before she comes out here with a paddle."

"I'm sorry," I said, backing away. "She isn't always like this."

"Don't worry about it. I'll call you later."

"Okay."

His eyes swept over me again. "Mm… I'd better get out of here before I kidnap you. Are you free after work?"

"I don't know. I have school tomorrow. Early."

"So is that a 'no'?"

Fuck it.

Krystal was right. I needed to get laid. It was time to find my own dark side. I smiled "Actually, it's a 'yes'. But only for a little while."

"Sweet. Call me when you're done working," he said, putting his sunglasses on. "We'll meet up."

"Okay."

Then he was gone and I was left to deal with my pissed off mother.

Sighing, I walked up to the house and opened the door, ready for a battle. It didn't take long.

"What are you doing with him?" she asked, looking disgusted.

"His name is Trevor and he's a nice guy," I replied, closing the door behind me.

"He's trash, Adriana."

"No, Mama, he's not. He's a good guy. You don't even know him."

"I know his kind and so do you. He's in a gang. A gang! I saw the patches on his jacket. Those are dangerous guys. Not what you need to be surrounding yourself with. I don't want you seeing him again."

I pursed my lips. "I'm an adult. I can make up my own mind on who I want to see."

She stared at me angrily. "So, what you are saying is that you *are* seeing him again? Even if I beg you not to?"

"Trevor is a great guy. You didn't even give him a chance."

"How can you do this, Adriana?" she asked me, looking tired and defeated. "You know what happened in Florida. What kind of people these bikers are. They are nothing but criminals."

"Trevor isn't a criminal. These guys are different, here. The Gold Vipers. It's not like it was in Florida. They are *nothing* like the Hell's Demons."

Her eyes narrowed. "Is that what he told you?"

"Well, not in so many words."

"Of course not. He wants you. You're a beautiful girl, Adriana. Men will say whatever you want to hear to get into your pants."

I bit back a smile. "I realize that. I'm not sixteen, though. I'm twenty-one."

"Yes. See. Just a babe."

Exasperated, I sighed. She would tell me this when I was thirty. That was her way.

Vanda wagged her index finger at me. "You realize that your father is probably turning in his grave right now, knowing that you're seeing this guy. How can you do that to him?"

"Papa's dead," I said. "But if he were alive, he'd at least give Trevor a chance."

"No," she said. "Never. Your father was almost killed because of a man like," she wrinkled her nose, "Trevor. I didn't tell you but, one of those bikers shot your father."

I stared at her in shock. "They did?"

She nodded. "Yes. He was shot in the shoulder. They wanted my wedding ring," she said, staring at her left hand, which had the replacement band. "The one that was handed down from his mother. It was two karats. Beautiful. After stealing almost all the jewelry in the shop, they demanded that, too."

"What happened?" I asked, my voice hollow. I hadn't heard that part of it. I knew they'd gotten the ring, but hadn't heard the actual story behind it.

She smiled sadly. "Your father, he was so sentimental. You remember? Always telling stories about your grandparents and their farm."

I nodded. My father's parents had traveled from Germany when he was a young boy. They moved to Iowa and bought a farm. This was several years before he met my mother, which was on a trip to Florida, after his mother had died of cancer. Vanda's family had also been immigrants. They'd moved from Portugal when she was a teenager to Miami. Her father, my grandfather, had been a wealthy jeweler, and that's where my mother had found her own passion for diamonds and gems. Eventually, my parents married and they opened up their first jewelry shop in Florida. "Yes. I remember."

She sighed. "He was so attached to that ring. It was an heirloom. A symbol of our marriage. Obviously, he didn't want them to have it. Told them they couldn't have it. Even told them why." Her lip quivered. "But, those ingrates didn't care and I could see right through them. I told your father that it was okay. That they could have the ring, but he kept arguing. Well, they shot him before I could get the ring even off of my finger. Then, they laughed when it was over. Made fun of your father, lying there bleeding and dying. Can you believe such evilness?"

"No," I whispered, imaging the horror. It made me sick to my stomach.

"So, you see, those are the kind of people you're dealing with. The kind that join these 'gangs'," she said, her face darkening.

"Why didn't you tell me about that?"

"You were only twelve and he didn't want you to know. Didn't want you to be frightened."

I sighed.

"Adriana," she said, grabbing my hand. "There are so many good boys out there. Don't waste your time with this guy. You'll regret it later. You'll be hurt, in one way or another."

"Mama…"

"Just, please…" She squeezed my hand. "Think about it, okay? For your father's sake, at least?"

I let out a ragged sigh. "Yes. I will definitely think about it."

She leaned forward and kissed my cheek. "You are all I have," she said, her eyes shining with tears. "I don't want to lose you, too."

"You won't," I said softly.

"Remember what you father used to say? You can't predict your own destiny, but you're responsible for choosing the path that leads you to it."

"I know, Mama. I know."

Chapter Fifteen

RAPTOR

After I left Adriana, I took a cruise on my bike to clear both of my heads, and then headed to Griffin's. I met up with Tank in the parking lot; there were shadows under his eyes and he looked like he hadn't slept in a week.

"Hey, man," I said, shoving my key into the front of my jeans. "You're looking pretty rough."

He shrugged. "Couldn't sleep."

"Even after I called you?"

He opened the door to the bar and we went inside. "Fuck no. I heard Krystal's phone go off right after we hung up, and when I read the text message sent to her, I was too jacked up to sleep."

"Message? What message?"

"Some douchebag named Gary sent her a message. It said, 'Thanks for everything'."

"Oh yeah? Did you ask her about it?"

"No."

"Why not?" I said, thinking the message could have meant anything.

"I was too pissed off. I mean, what kind of asshole sends a girl a message at four in the morning? Like he can't get her out of his mind." He rubbed a hand over his face. "I needed time to think."

"Could be nothing," I thought, knowing that it could also be a lot. After getting screwed over by Brandy, I wasn't sure what to believe myself. "She ever mention a guy named Gary?"

"No. Not at all."

"You know you gotta ask her."

"I know." He sighed. "I don't know. I'm almost tempted to just say 'fuck it' and find some new pussy. I don't like this feeling jealous kind of shit. Too many girls willing to keep me satisfied, you know? Without the baggage or the worries."

"I feel you, brother. I wish I'd have never met Brandy. She was bad news. "

Two of the club whores walked by us as we sauntered over to the bar.

"Hey, Raptor, looking good," said Cheeks, who I'd banged a couple of times. "You need some company later, let me know."

"Will do," I said, staring at her ass as she walked away. I had to admit – it was as nice as fuck, hence her nickname, but it didn't compare to Adriana's. Not from what I'd seen in those tight jeans of hers or felt under my fingertips. I imagined her wearing a G-string and my dick perked up again.

"Fuck," I muttered, adjusting myself.

"What's wrong?"

"Nothing."

Tank tapped his fingers on the bar impatiently. "You know, I should just go and fuck the shit out of the new chick," he said, eyeing the curvy blonde on stage with the big plastic tits. She was in her thirties and not much to look at above the neck, but even I had to admit, she knew how to work the poles. She'd shown me just how well, the week before. "Take my mind off of all the shit for a while."

"Just don't be late for the meeting, or your old man will have your balls," I said as the bartender, Misty, set two icy-cold beers in front of us.

"No shit. Last time I was late, I thought he was going to have a fucking heart-attack, he was so pissed off. Wasn't even my fault that I got a flat tire."

"That's because it was flat the night before, and he knew it," I reminded him and then winked at Misty. "Thanks, darlin'"

Misty tossed her jet black hair over her shoulder and smiled. "Anytime, Raptor. Just so you know, the kitchen is open. You boys want me to put in an order for you?"

Tank's lip curled up. "I'll take an order of you, lovely lady."

Misty laughed. "Really? And what about your pretty little blond, Krystal?"

"What about her?" he asked, reaching over the bar to grab a toothpick. "You thinking about a threesome?"

She giggled. "You are so bad."

"Baby, you have no idea."

Still smiling, she turned to me. "So, you hungry or what, Raptor?"

"I've already eaten," I said, taking a swig of beer.

"To be honest, I haven't eaten yet," said Tank, wiggling his eyebrows. "And what I'm craving isn't on the menu."

She leaned forward on the bar, her tits bulging out of her halter top. "And what is it you're craving?" she asked seductively.

"Whatever you're serving," he said, staring at her chest.

Misty lowered her voice. "What if I'm willing to serve you both? At once."

Tank chuckled and looked at me. "You game? I'll take the front and you can have the back."

"No thanks. She's all yours."

"You sure?" pouted Misty, grabbing my hand. She put it on her left tit. "I'll let you fuck me in the ass."

Laughing, I removed it. "Tank, you've got your hands full."

He took a swig of his beer. "Does that offer stand for me, too?"

She winked at him. "Honey, I've had you inside of me and I know what you're made of. I don't need any trips to the E.R."

Slammer walked out of the back room and scowled. "Put your dick back into your pants, Tank, and meet me in my office. We need to talk. You too, Raptor."

Tank straightened up. "Can't it wait?"

"Nope. Misty, can you put an order in for a burger and onion rings?"

"Sure thing, Slammer," she said, hurrying toward the kitchen.

He stopped next to us. "You two should stay away from Misty," said Slammer in a low voice. "Girl's crazy. She even fucked that asshole, Breaker, last night."

Tank's eyes narrowed. "No shit? What the fuck?"

"She told me she only did it to see if she could get some information. Like she's some kind of secret agent on a mission." He pointed to his head. "I admire her loyalty to the club, but the girl's not all fucking there."

"He could have messed her up pretty badly," I answered.

"She probably wouldn't care. In fact, she likes it rough," said Tank, smiling grimly. "Asked me to choke her once."

Slammer grunted. "Doesn't surprise me."

"Did you?" I asked, as Tank leaned against the bar again and watched the stage.

He shook his head. "Honestly, I tried and then stopped when she kept begging me to do it harder. I just felt too weird about it. I like rough sex as much as the next guy, but the choking thing, that's fucked up."

"She's one loony bitch. You want your dick waxed, stick with Bunny, Shy, or Cheeks. They won't kill you in your sleep," said Slammer as Misty walked back out of the kitchen.

"The order is in. You want me to bring it back to your office when it's done?"

Slammer looked around the bar. It was dead. "That or send Blue back with it. I know he's here somewhere."

"He took a magazine into the bathroom," said Misty, nodding toward the restrooms. "He's been in there for a while."

Slammer scowled. "Fuck. Okay, you bring me the food," he said, walking back toward his office.

"You want to meet up later?" Misty asked Tank, as we were preparing to follow him.

"No. Gonna head out to the club after this. We've got church at three."

"I know. Text me later tonight if you change your mind." She looked at me and winked. "Either of you. I'm game for whatever you want."

Disturbed by the fact that she'd screwed Breaker, I grabbed my beer and followed Tank into Slammer's office.

"Close the door," said Slammer, sitting down behind his desk.

Tank did. "What's up?"

I sat down across from Slammer and noticed he had a file on his desk.

Slammer lit a cigarette and waited until Tank was in the other chair. He leaned back. "Mud still isn't backing down."

"I didn't think he would. Breaker's his nephew," said Tank.

"I know, but what's right is right. Letting Breaker get away with raping my future stepdaughter, is a punch in the face. I know he did it. Mud knows he did it. I need vindication."

"So, you're absolutely sure it wasn't one of the other Devil's Rangers?" asked Tank.

"Oh, fuck yeah," said Slammer, who was looking every bit of his fifty-seven years. He rubbed the gray stubble on his chin and sighed. "Jessica saw the patches on his cut. It was theirs."

"She remember anything else?" I asked.

"To be honest, she won't even talk to me. Just to Frannie. But, the description she gave fits. And we all know what a fucking whack-job Breaker is."

"This was personal," said Tank, staring at his beer bottle. "I know it was. He must have known who she was."

"I agree," said Slammer. "And I'm not letting that sonofabitch get away it."

"What are you going to do?" I asked.

"I've ordered a hit on him," he said, opening up the folder. Inside was a picture of Breaker and a sheet of paper with his address and other personal information scribbled across it. "I need you to deliver this to our guy."

"Why don't we just do it ourselves and get it over with?" asked Tank.

"That's what they're expecting. We do this out in the open, there will be an all-out war. It has to look like something else."

"So what?" he said, his eyes hardening. "We need to send them a fucking message. All of them."

"I agree, son. You know I do. But," he blew out a cloud of smoke. "I'm getting married soon, and

I promised Frannie that I wouldn't land my ass in jail. I don't want either of you going, either. Not for that bozo."

"So, who's going to do it? The Judge?" I asked.

He nodded. "I don't want anyone else to know about it, though. Not even the rest of the crew."

"Why not let them in on it?" asked Tank. "They're going to figure out you had something to do with it anyway."

"Can't do that."

"Why?" I asked. Slammer never made any decisions like this without letting the others know about it first. Of course, he didn't order many hits on people, either. This was only the second one I'd heard of.

"I think one of them is an informant."

"A cop?" I asked.

He grunted. "No, not that. A stoolpigeon. For Mud."

"How did you come to that conclusion?" asked Tank.

"Information has been leaked. Information that neither of you even know about."

"What the fuck does that mean?" asked Tank, looking pissed.

"Mud asked me how to get in touch with Jordan Steele. He shouldn't even know that we're connected. That I've ever had any business with him."

"Who is this Jordan Steele?" I asked. I'd never heard of him.

Slammer looked me straight in the eye. "Your brother. The Judge."

Chapter Sixteen

Adriana

My mother went back to the shop to check on business, and I took a shower. When I was finished and blow-drying my hair, Tiffany called me.

"Holy crap, I just heard what happened," she said. "That fucking asshole."

I walked into my bedroom and started searching for something to wear. "I know," I replied, pulling out a black cashmere sweater from the dresser. I threw it on the bed next to my new white denim skirt, and decided they'd look good together.

"Did you call the police?"

"No," I replied, rifling through my underwear drawer. I held up a white silk thong, one that I'd purchased one a whim, and decided to pair it with a black and white pushup bra.

It's not for Trevor, I told myself.

In fact, I'd decided not to meet with him later. No matter how sexy and sweet he'd been, I didn't need to get involved with someone who had admitted that he was some kind of an outlaw. Especially after what my mother had told me. Even if it was just for sex. Amazing sex.

"Why not?" she screeched. "That guy should be locked up!"

"It's going to be taken care of," I said, remembering Trevor's words.

"What does that mean?"

I sighed. "I think he's going to be roughed up."

She was silent for a few seconds and then laughed. "You can't be serious? By who? Oh, wait… by Tank and his biker friends?"

"Something like that."

"I doubt that's going to help. It might scare him, for a while, but only really sick fuckers do that kind of stuff. He'll start up again eventually. Seriously, Adriana, Jason needs to be locked up before he rapes some other poor, unsuspecting girl."

"Easier said than done. I don't have any real proof that *he* did anything," I answered.

"You were drugged. That's evidence enough."

"Yeah, well, I didn't see him do it, and I'm sure I don't have any more of it in my system. I don't know if you heard, but I threw up all over him before he could even get my sweater off."

She burst out laughing. "Oh, my God, I know it's not funny but… I'm just picturing his face when you puked all over him. That must have been priceless."

I smiled. It was scary at the time, but thinking back, he deserved that and so much more. "He was pretty pissed. Great timing on my part, though."

"Obviously it couldn't have been any more perfect," she agreed.

"I just wish it would have happened before I got in the car with him. He dropped me off in the middle of nowhere and I had to call Tank's friend for a ride."

"Tank's friend?"

"Well, I tried calling you," I replied, not ready to tell her too much about Trevor yet. After the conversation with my mother, I wasn't too sure about him myself anymore.

"I know, I'm sorry. I actually ended up going over to Jeff's. I told Krystal, but she forgot."

Jeff was a guy she sometimes hooked up with after clubbing. They used to date in high school.

"It's okay."

"You know, I wonder if the other guys were in on it," said Tiffany, sounding angry again. "Gary and Brian. And... what was that other guy's name? Lucas?"

"Yeah, that's it. I don't know if they knew about it."

"Fucking assholes."

"Have you ever seen any of them before?" I asked, knowing she hung out at the clubs frequently.

"Not that I remember. I mean, it's possible, I guess. I may have just never noticed those guys.

My phone vibrated. "I gotta go," I told her. "It looks like my mom's trying to get ahold of me."

"Okay. Call me later."

"I will."

I hung up and called my mother back.

"Can you come in a little earlier?" she asked. "Gerald's got a migraine and we're swamped. I need you to take customers."

"I'll be there within the hour," I told her.

"Thanks, Adriana."

"No, problem."

We hung up and I exchanged the sweater and white skirt for a short-sleeved black dress, knowing that my parents had always preferred their salespeople to dress more formally.

As I was putting my hair up, I thought about my father and how much I missed him. He'd been our rock and had spoiled me rotten growing up. The thought of someone shooting him and then laughing about it brought tears to my eyes.

How could anyone give such little regard to a man's life?

Especially someone who was so much more than what those robbers had been. My father had been a kind man. A decent man. He'd been involved with the community and had given to charities. He'd even volunteered his time at the local shelter during the holidays to remind himself that anyone could fall into hard times.

"It could happen to any of us," he once said to my mother when she'd first complained about him leaving us on Christmas Eve to volunteer. "One day you have everything, the next, you lose your job and struggle to put food on the table for your children. Look at the presents under our tree, Vanda. Imagine that there's nothing there. *Nothing.* Or nothing in the refrigerator. No ham. No turkey. Not even a piece of bologna. Then, imagine what it's like to have to look into your child's face and tell them that there is no Santa Claus because you can't afford to buy them a gift, let alone a full meal." Then she said he'd grabbed the credit card and went to buy as many toys as he could carry to the shelter after purchasing a Santa Claus suit. It became a tradition, and the following year Vanda began to help him while I stayed behind with my grandparents, not having a clue as to what they were doing. Then, when I was old enough to understand, I helped wrap presents and even went with to deliver them. It wasn't until we moved to Iowa, after they'd been robbed, that things changed and the volunteering stopped. Dad was diagnosed with lymphoma and his health began to deteriorate rapidly. Despite chemotherapy and trying other kinds of homeopathic treatments, he had died within eighteen months.

    Remembering our last moments together, I went into the safe under my bed and took out the necklace my mother had given to me when I'd graduated high school. The one that my father had designed for the occasion, but hadn't lived to see it. It was chunky, with white-gold chains, and a round pendant that contained a large dark blue sapphire. My birthstone. The gem itself had to be close to ten karats, and worth more than my new car.

I put the necklace on and blinked away the tears in my eyes. I decided to wear it to work. Not only in honor of my father, but as a reminder to why I needed to stay away from Trevor, no matter how hard it was to resist that sexy, blond biker.

Chapter Seventeen

RAPTOR

"What the fuck you just say?" I asked, staring at him in shock.

Slammer smiled grimly. "He's your half-brother."

"My mom had another kid?"

"Yeah. This was long before Mavis and your old man hooked-up. About six years before that time, I believe."

My heart was pounding in my chest. *I had a fucking brother?* "How come I never heard about him?"

"She was probably too scared to say anything around your father. He beat the shit out of her enough as it was."

"Is that why she took off?" I asked, feeling a lump in my throat. Did she take off to be with her first son, while leaving me behind?

"She left to get away from your father. She knew I'd take care of you. I told her I would and she trusted me. She's my second cousin. Did you know that?"

"Yeah, I think you mentioned that before," I said, staring blindly down at his desk as the shit sunk in.

"Anyway, Mavis took off but she didn't even try to collect Jordan. She knew better than that. Plus, he was an adult by then. Nineteen, I think."

"Who's Jordan's father?" I asked, looking up at him.

"His name is Acid and he's from California. Part of the Demon Rebels. I think their chapter is located in Sacramento, but I'm not totally sure. Never had any dealings with any of them."

"Acid," repeated Tank. His eyes widened. "Holy shit, I know who you're talking about. I saw something about him on the news last year. I think he's doing time for arson, or some other shit."

"Oh, he's doing time, but it's not where you think," said Slammer, smirking. "That fucker is dead."

"What do you mean?" I asked, still in shock that The Judge was my older brother.

"You can ask The Judge about it," he replied, nodding toward the folder. "When you give him this and the cash. Which reminds me." He walked to the safe and opened it up. "The money is in here," he said, holding up a large padded envelope. "Ten thousand dollars. Make sure he gets all of that or we're fucked."

Tank whistled. "You sure you don't want me to take care of Breaker? I'll do it for half."

"Sorry, but we just can't risk it."

Tank frowned but didn't say anything.

"Ten thousand, huh?" I said, as he handed the package to me. "So, does he know about me?"

"Yep."

That knowledge kind of pissed me off. "He knows about me. So, why don't I know about him?"

"I made a promise to your mother. Hell, she pretty much begged me not to say anything to you. She wanted to wait until the right time to tell you herself."

"And when would that be?" I mumbled. "On her deathbed? I don't have any contact with her as it is. Fuck, I don't even know *where* she is."

"She's in town, actually," he said.

I didn't say anything for a while. The bitterness I felt for Mavis abandoning me still gnawed at me at times. I didn't even want to hear any more about her. "How come Jordan's never tried getting in touch?" I asked, changing the subject to him.

Slammer took a few seconds to answer. "Let's just say that I don't think Acid was an easy man to live with and now Jordan doesn't have much empathy for family, and from what I can tell, he's a cold sonofabitch himself. He even refused to meet your mother."

"From what I've heard, he's a loner," said Tank. "In fact, I heard that he hates people. All people."

"Maybe not. Maybe so. Whatever the case may be, he *is* a mercenary and having friends and family would be more of a liability."

"Yeah, I get it. So, who all knows about him?" I asked, wondering where the leak was coming from.

"Up until a few weeks ago, only your mother and I knew who The Judge really was. But, then she showed up here, asking me to set up a meeting between the two of them. To be honest, I think she wanted to have him do a job for her. Anyway, when he said 'no', she got drunk and whined about it to a couple of our brothers. Later that night, they approached me about it, and I had to come clean. I told them to keep their fucking mouths shut, though. Obviously one of them didn't. Horse. Well, he told Chopper, and Chopper told Buck, and you get the idea… Anyway, the last I checked, everyone but you two knew about it."

"Fuck," said Tank, shaking his head. "That got out of hand pretty quickly. And why the fuck didn't you tell me? I'm your second-in-command. Not to mention your son."

"I just did."

Tank snorted. "Still, it's easy to see how Mud learned about it. I doubt there's a fucking conspiracy."

"They all gave me their solemn word that nobody else would find out about it. Nobody. And that they'd keep their fucking mouths shut," said Slammer.

"They probably told their Old Ladies, and that's how it leaked," I said. "You know most of them are always running their mouths about this thing or that."

"Exactly and that's why I warned them about keeping it quiet. From what I gathered, none of the Old Ladies know about it, either."

"Still, I don't know," said Tank. "They may have promised, but shit happens. People get drunk and talk shit. Do we have a traitor in our group? I don't know. More than likely, it's just a couple of guys who can't hold their liquor. Don't get me wrong, I'd kick their ass if I found out who leaked it."

Slammer sighed and rubbed the bridge of his nose. "I know. It's why nobody else is going to learn about the hit on Breaker. Nobody. Got it?"

"Of course," I said.

Tank nodded.

"When did Mavis find out about The Judge?" I asked.

Slammer frowned. "Well, to tell you the truth, I fucked that up myself a couple of years ago. She was over at the house and we were sharing a bottle of Cuervo Gold. We started talking about you and then Jordan and Acid. Said she didn't even know if Jordan was alive, since he'd basically disappeared off of the face of the earth. That's when I told her."

"Mavis was over at *our* house?" asked Tank. He looked at me to see my reaction. "Thought she was the one who'd disappeared off the face of the earth."

"No, shit," I said.

"I know. I know." Slammer rocked back on his chair. "Look, there's something I never told you, but Mavis dropped by quite a bit, asking about you."

"I didn't know that. Funny, she could have just come to me directly," I said dryly.

"She was scared and confused." He sighed. "I hate to say this but with all of the beatings your mother took over the years, she's not the same person I once knew. I mean, she always had a drinking problem and hung out with some real assholes, but now… let's just say that she's not all there. Not mentally."

I gave him a disgusted look. "I wouldn't know the real Mavis. She kept her distance from me, even when I was a kid," I muttered, thinking back to my childhood. The fighting. The drinking. Even the drugs. The closest thing I had to a real home was living with Slammer and Tank. I certainly wasn't going to hold a grudge against him because he never said anything. He had his reasons.

I sighed. "So, where is she living now?"

"I guess she's been staying with a girlfriend."

"And she wants to hire 'The Judge' for a hit?"

"That's what I'm guessing," said Slammer.

"You know who?" I asked.

"Not too sure. You hear from Butch lately?" he asked, smirking. "That would be my first guess."

My old man, Butch, was in prison for drug smuggling. "Nope. Just that time two years ago when he asked me for some money. Said I owed him because he gave me life."

Tank grunted. "What a fucking prick. You didn't give him any, did you?"

I shook my head and smiled. "I gave him what I felt he deserved. My middle finger."

Slammer's cell phone went off. He picked it up and looked at the screen. "It's Frannie. I need to take this call."

"So, how do I reach Jordan?" I asked.

"He'll contact you. I gave him your number. And, for fuck's sake, don't call him Jordan. Call him Judge. Hey, darlin'," he said, answering the phone. I had to smile when I noticed his voice rise to a higher tone.

Tank nodded toward me and we got up and left the office.

"Remember what I said about keeping your mouths shut!" hollered Slammer as we walked down the hallway. "And don't miss church!"

"You want me to head out with you?" asked Tank, as we stepped back into the bar. "Make sure that money stays safe."

I patted the envelope. "It's safe with me. Besides, didn't you want a piece of Misty?" I asked, nodding toward the bartender, who was waiting on a couple of regulars.

"Fuck no. You heard what the old man said. I'm not going near that shit. Not after Breaker infected it." He sighed. "In fact, I'm going to call Krystal. Make sure it's still on for tonight. You still want to go and hunt that fucker down, don't you?"

"Jason? Yeah. He needs some guidance counseling."

Tank grunted. "No shit."

"I'll meet you at the clubhouse," I said, walking toward the doorway with the file. "I've got a couple of errands to run, first."

"Okay, brother."

Chapter Eighteen

Adriana

When I finished putting my makeup on, I slipped on a pair of black pumps and a lightweight overcoat. Then I locked the house up and walked over to the garage where my Verano was parked. When I started the engine, I noticed I was getting low on fuel, so on the way to Dazzle, I stopped at a fuel station. I'd just started pumping gas when I noticed that a big, black truck had pulled up behind my car. Ignoring it, I continued filling my car with gasoline.

The person in the truck got out and I heard footsteps come up behind me. "Darlin', I thought that was you," said a gravelly voice.

I turned around to find myself looking up into the cold, flat eyes of the biker who'd been harassing me at Griffin's. Breaker. I tried to remain calm.

"Sorry?" I said, pretending I didn't know him. The guy was even scarier in the daylight, the scar on his face standing out like a warning sign. Something told me that he'd probably deserved it.

"You're the hot little number from Griffin's last night. You must remember me, darlin'."

My heart was pounding as I pulled the nozzle out of the car and shoved it back into the machine. I'd barely filled my tank, but I wanted to leave as quickly as possible. Knowing that he'd gone to prison for rape was terrifying. Especially since he was obviously still interested in me. "Sorry. You must have me confused with someone else," I answered, laughing nervously. "I get that all the time."

He smirked. "I don't think so."

Ignoring him, I pulled out my receipt and tried getting into my car.

"You know, I'd never forget a face like yours," he said, blocking my way.

"Excuse me. You're in my way."

His eyes went to my necklace. "Fuck me, is that a real sapphire?"

I put my hand over the stone. "No. Of course not. It's costume jewelry. Now, if you'd please get out of my way, I really have to be somewhere."

"Are you okay, honey?" asked a little old lady, pumping gas across from me.

"Mind your own business, grandma," said Breaker, stepping out of my way.

The woman quickly turned away and continued pumping.

"Nosy old bitch," he muttered and then turned back to me. "You meeting up with Raptor?"

I ignored him.

He chuckled. "You look like you're going on a date. He's not going to be happy knowing that you're seeing someone on the side."

I was about to tell him that I wasn't seeing anyone, including Raptor, but caught myself. That would have been asking for more trouble. I forced a grin. "For your information, I'm going to work but I *will* be seeing him later."

He grinned slyly. "Work, huh? Where you work, darlin'?"

I couldn't help it. I was tired of his questions. "It's none of your business," I said, slamming the door shut. I quickly started the engine and locked all four doors. As I backed away, I noticed that he was laughing.

"Asshole," I mumbled, turning the car around. I drove out of the parking lot and headed down the road, still shaken. The light ahead turned red and I slowed down to a stop. As I waited for it to change, someone revved their engine behind me. I looked into my rearview mirror and my blood ran cold. Breaker was behind me, in the truck, and only inches from my bumper.

I swore under my breath, hoping that he wasn't following me and just heading north. But, common sense told me that was not the case.

When the light finally changed, I began to drive forward, but didn't head toward Dazzle, which was only a few blocks away. The last thing I needed was for him to learn where I worked. Instead, I continued forward, not exactly sure where I was headed. Frustratingly enough, he stayed behind me for the next five lights.

Shit, he must really be following me, I thought, deciding to take a right at the next light. As I put my blinker on and changed lanes, I noticed he did the same. We both turned on the green arrow, and I looked back at him in my rearview mirror. I couldn't see his face because the windows were tinted, but something told me he was enjoying this. Tightening my hands on the wheel, I sped up and took the next exit, this time turning left. He quickly followed.

"Dammit," I snapped, my heart racing. I reached into my purse, which was sitting next to me on the seat, and grabbed my cell phone. Trying not to get into an accident, I quickly dialed Trevor.

"Hey, Kitten," he answered, a smile in his voice. "I didn't expect to hear from you until later."

"Breaker is following me," I said quickly.

He swore. "Talk to me."

I told him about seeing Breaker at the gas station and how he'd tried talking to me. "Now he's on my tail."

"I'm going to kill that fucking asshole myself. Swear to God," he growled. "Okay. Where are you?"

I gave him my approximate location. "Should I drive to the nearest police station?" I asked, still seeing Breaker's truck in my mirror.

"He'll just drive away if you do that."

"Isn't that the point?" I exclaimed loudly.

"I want to confront the fucker. Let him know that nobody follows my girl."

I'm not your girl, I thought, although I had to admit that part of me was giddy at the comment. "Seriously, I don't want to be part of that. I just want him to go away and never see him again."

"I know, but shitheads like Breaker *won't* go away unless someone stands up to them. Look," he said, "why don't you head on over to Griffin's? You're only ten minutes away. I'm in the parking lot, now. *I'll* make sure that pile of shit never bothers you again. You feel me?"

I was feeling more frustrated than anything as I stopped at another light. This time, however, Breaker got into the right turning lane. "Wait a second," I said, looking over at his truck. "He's turning away. Thank God."

Breaker rolled down his window and the menacing smile on his face gave me the chills. He blew me a kiss and then drove away, his tires squealing as he whipped around the corner.

"Asshole," I mumbled, sighing in relief.

"What's going on?"

"He's gone."

"Good. Now, meet me at Griffin's. I'll take you to lunch."

Yuck, like I'd ever eat there.

"I can't. My mom's expecting me at the store. I'm surprised she hasn't called me yet, complaining."

He was quiet for a while, obviously mulling things over. "Okay. You get your ass at work and don't worry your pretty little head about this jerkoff."

"Thanks," I said. "He scared the crap out of me."

"Don't let him, Kitten. In fact, he won't be bothering anyone soon."

"Oh yeah? Why?"

"I can't get into it. Just, go to work and I'll see you later tonight."

I bit my lower lip. "About that…"

"I've gotta go. There's a call coming in. I might even meet you at Dazzle, later." He chuckled. "Surprise your mother."

"But –"

"Later, babe," he said and then hung up.

Sighing, I tossed my phone onto the passenger seat and headed to the shop, checking my rearview mirror frequently. I couldn't believe the last twenty-four hours, I'd had strange encounters with three very different guys. As far as I was concerned, every one of them was a threat. Even Trevor.

Chapter Nineteen

RAPTOR

"This Raptor?" asked the voice on the other end.

"Yeah."

"You've got a package for me?"

I glanced at my saddlebag. "I do."

"Meet me at your house. In twenty minutes," he said and then hung up.

He knew where I lived. I wasn't sure how I felt about that. Yeah, we were brothers, but he was still The Judge and something told me that blood meant nothing to him, unless he was getting paid to spill it.

Sighing, I got on my bike and tied a red and white bandana around my head. Then I headed home.

***

Adriana

"Oh good. You're here," said my mother, as I stepped into the busy shop. She was showing a young couple some diamond engagement rings. "I sent Gerald home already. Could you help Mrs. Jacobs clean her jewelry?" She nodded toward the back of the shop where and elderly woman was waiting. "Tim and I are both just too busy at the moment."

I looked across the room at Tim, who many said looked like Zac Efron's twin brother. He was surrounded by three teenaged girls who appeared to be interested in both the charm bracelets and the young guy behind the counter.

"Sure. No problem."

"Hi, Adriana," said Tim as I walked by him. He looked at me over his shoulder and gave me dimpled smile.

"Hi, Tim."

"You look lovely today. Hey," he squinted. "Is that a new necklace? It's gorgeous."

"It's not new. By the way, you're looking pretty swanky yourself. Tell whoever's dressing you that they have amazing taste."

He winked. "I certainly will." As usual, he was dressed to the nines in a black tailored suit. His boyfriend, Juan, worked at Macy's, and had excellent taste in fashion. From what I understood, he selected all of Tim's clothes and wouldn't let him step out of the house without approving his clothing choices.

I hung up my coat on the hook behind the counter, and began helping Mrs. Jacobs. When her jewelry was cleaned, she asked to look at some earrings that were in the case.

"These are so lovely," she said, trying on a set of pearl ones. "I keep looking at them every time I visit your shop." She sighed. "I should just get them."

"I would. They're beautiful, and they're not lab-created," I told her. "Hence the price. You're going to pay for quality and Vanda goes to great lengths to make sure we sell the finest pearl earrings in Iowa."

"Yes, I believe it. I do know that you get what you pay for, too. I've learned that over the years."

I nodded.

"The price is reasonable. I keep waiting for them to go down, though."

"We had a sale last week," I whispered, leaning forward. "Twenty percent off. If you want the earrings, I'll do what I can to get you that same deal. I know the owner and I'm pretty sure she'll okay it."

She smiled. "If you can do that, I'll take them, for sure."

I winked. "Let's wrap them up so you can take them home."

"Thank you, Adriana. I'm going to tell your boss that you're a 'keeper'."

I laughed. "Thank you. Hopefully, she'll believe you."

"You two are having fun over here," said Vanda, walking over to us after ringing up her couple. "I like that."

"A happy customer is a return customer," said Mrs. Jacobs. "And you know, I keep coming back."

"And we are thrilled that you do," she replied and then looked down at the earrings. "Ah, you're getting them. The ones you've been eyeing for weeks. I just marked them down, too. Perfect timing."

My eyes widened. "You did?"

"Yes," she replied. "I took twenty-percent off last night."

"So, I'm getting forty-percent off of the original price?" raved Mrs. Jacobs, grinning. "My goodness. This is really my day!"

My mother's eyebrows shot up and she looked at me.

I laughed nervously. "I promised her twenty-percent off the current price. Sorry, I didn't know you'd already lowered it."

I could tell by the look in her eyes that she wasn't too happy with me, but she faked it for Mrs. Jacobs. "It's quite all right." She winked at the older woman. "I guess this *is* your lucky day, isn't it? Well, I don't know who deserves it more than you. I really do appreciate all of the business you've given me, Mrs. Jacobs. All of us do."

"Call me Mary."

"Mary. Thank you, Mary," she replied.

The phone in the store rang and Tim answered it.

"Adriana, it's for you," he said, putting the caller on hold.

"I'm with a customer," I said. "Can you take a message?"

"It's okay. I'll ring her up," said my mother. "Take your call."

"Thanks," I said. "Enjoy your earrings, Mary. They look lovely on your ears."

She touched her ears. "Thank you, Adriana."

Smiling, I walked over and grabbed the phone.

"Hello?"

The caller didn't say anything.

"Hello? This is Adriana. Can I help you?"

I heard the distinct sound of a lighter being flicked. Then someone inhaled what I could only imagine to be a cigarette. Then they blew it out.

"Hello?" I said, getting frustrated. "I'm going to hang up if you've got nothing to say to me."

The sound of man's deep laughter made my blood turn cold.

I gripped the phone tightly. "Who is this?"

The person hung up.

My hand was shaking when I placed the phone back on the receiver. I knew who it was. I could tell by his coarse, evil laughter.

Breaker.

"Who was that?" asked Tim, looking concerned.

I forced a smile. "Wrong number."

"That's strange because the man actually asked for you."

"Huh," I said, moving around the counter and toward the front of the shop.

"Where you going?" called my mom.

I didn't reply. I walked to the front door and glanced outside, terrified of what I'd find.

"Is there something wrong?" asked Jim Evans, our security guard.

"I don't know," I said, looking around the parking lot. There were six cars, including mine, but no menacing black truck. I relaxed a little.

Jim stood up. "You're worrying me, Adriana," he said, looking out the window himself. "Is there something we should know?"

He was like a hawk. He noticed everything and trusted nobody, outside of my mother and me. He even had a hard time trusting Tim and Gerald. It made him an excellent security guard. "No," I replied, turning to him. "Everything is fine. Really."

At least I hoped.

Vanda approached us. "What's wrong?" she whispered frantically. "Why didn't you answer me?"

"I'm sorry and nothing is wrong, Mom."

She didn't look like she believed me. "Who was on the phone? Tim said you looked like you'd seen a ghost."

I managed a smile. "Oh, well that was just a crank call. Some punk kid. Where is Mrs. Jacobs?" I asked, looking behind her.

"Bathroom. I think she's used it more than me," said Vanda, chuckling.

"That's what happens when you get old," said Jim, who was pushing fifty himself. "Leaky faucets and rusty pipes."

"You're not old," replied Mom. "And I'm sure your pipes are working just fine."

His face turned red and he smiled. "Easy for you to say. You look like Adriana's sister, not mother."

"Flattery will get you ten-percent over cost on something for your own mother," she replied, grinning. "Come Mother's Day."

He laughed. "I'll hold you to it."

Vanda chuckled.

"I'm going into the back for a quick cup of coffee. Would either of you ladies like me to grab you any?" he asked.

"No," I replied. "I'm fine."

"No, thank you, Jim," said Vanda. "I've had enough cups myself today."

"Let me know if you change your mind," he said, walking away.

Vanda watched him leave and then turned to me. "Oh," she said, reaching over to my necklace. She lifted up the sapphire. "You wore your father's necklace. It's been a long time since I've seen it."

I looked down. "I guess I couldn't stop thinking about Dad this morning."

Her eyes grew moist and she smiled. "He was such a good man."

"He was. The best."

She looked outside again and then back to my necklace. "I must admit, it makes me a little nervous –

you wearing it out in the open. It's very expensive and not exactly... subtle."

"I know. I probably shouldn't have," I admitted. "It's just... I wanted to feel close to him today."

"I understand," she replied, glancing down at her wedding band that she refused to remove, even though he'd been gone for the last seven years. "I wouldn't dream of taking this off."

"I'm sure if you did, though, Dad would be okay with it."

Her eyes widened. "Why would I ever take it off?"

I shrugged. "I don't know... I mean, you're only forty-seven. You might fall in love again."

"I've been in love. I don't need to replace your father."

"Don't you get lonely?" I asked.

She patted me on the shoulder and turned to walk away. "I have you, Adriana. I'm never lonely."

"I know, but –"

"Let it rest," she interrupted. "We've been through this conversation before. I'm content with my life."

I sighed. We *had* been through it before and she was always so stubborn. I knew if she opened her eyes, she'd see that Jim had a thing for her. But, that was Vanda. She was so obstinate.

The phone rang again and I jumped. This time, fortunately, it was for Tim.

Chapter Twenty

Raptor

When I arrived home, I left my bike in the driveway, unlocked the door, and went inside. When I reached the kitchen, a man was waiting for me at the table. He was dressed in a long, black leather overcoat and wore gloves.

"You Raptor?" he asked pointing his nine millimeter at me.

"Yeah, who the fuck are you?"

He put the gun down on the table. "You're smart. Figure it out."

"Jesus Christ, how the fuck did you get in here?" I snapped, not too happy that he'd made himself at home and was drinking one of my beers.

The Judge, who had dark hair and light blue eyes, smirked. "Back door. Used the key hidden under the pot with the dead Begonias. Did anyone ever tell you to water your flowers?"

I frowned. "I didn't hide a spare key there."

"Then you'd better figure out who did."

Brandy.

It had to be her. It was even her flower pot.

"I need to change my fucking locks," I said, staring at him, trying to find some kind of resemblance. From what I could see, there wasn't anything other than maybe the eye color.

"That mine?" he asked, nodding to the package in my arm.

"Yeah." I handed it to him. "It's all there."

He opened it up and pulled out the folder with Breaker's information. "I don't need this," he said, tossing it aside. Then he pulled out the bundles of money and counted them. "Looks like it's all here," he said before standing up.

"So, when are you going to do it?"

"Do what?" he asked, walking toward the kitchen door.

"Kill the fucker?"

He stopped abruptly and then turned around to face me. His smile was cold. "Don't know what you're talking about. Murder is a crime, kid. You should know that."

"I'm not your fucking 'kid'," I said, not appreciating his condescending bullshit.

"Relax, *brother*," he said, smirking again. "Didn't your daddy ever teach you the importance of self-control?"

"My old man's idea of self-control was waiting until seven a.m. for his first shot of whiskey," I said. "From what I hear, your old man wasn't much better, *Jordan*."

I thought he'd be pissed, but instead, he surprised me. "See, that's where you're wrong," he replied, removing one of his gloves. He lifted his right hand and even I had to wince at the scars. "He demanded self-control. As you can see, I learned it early on."

"That's from acid, isn't it?"

"Oh yeah," he said. "Looks like 'Dear Old Ma' sure knew how to pick 'em."

I smirked. "No shit. Have you met her?"

"No," he said, putting the glove back on. "And I really don't care to."

"I haven't seen her in years myself."

"Lucky you," he said, walking out of the kitchen.

I followed him. "What happens now?"

"I leave," he said, turning around. There was a look of mirth in his eyes. "Why?"

I shrugged. "I don't know. Did you want to ask me anything?"

"About what?"

"We're brothers. Thought you'd be curious."

"It's only blood, kid," he said, heading down the steps. "Don't get hung up on it."

I didn't know what else to say. It was obvious that he wasn't interested in shooting the shit, but that didn't stop me from being curious. "See you around?"

He grunted. "In my occupation, you'd better hope that you don't."

I stared at him.

He grinned and then left.

I pulled out my cell phone. "He's paid," I told Slammer.

"He say when it's going to happen?"

"No. In fact, he acted like he didn't know what the fuck I was even talking about when I asked him the same thing."

"That's the way he is. Okay, get your ass to the chapel. Meeting is going to start in thirty minutes."

"I'll be there."

He hung up.

I put my phone away and went around the house, checking the locks. Then I went outside and found the key he'd replaced under the flower pot. I stuck it in my pocket, threw the flower pot away, and left for the clubhouse.

***

Slammer smacked the gavel and called the meeting to order. There were nineteen of us in the Jensen Chapter, plus three prospects hoping to be patched. The prospects were absent, as they weren't allowed at the meetings for obvious reasons.

It was most of the same stuff, with the treasurer going over our finances, new correspondences, and then us voting on prospects. When that was finished, Slammer made a surprising announcement.

"You all have heard by now what happened to my Old Lady's daughter," he said, staring down at his folded hands. "And about my meeting with Mud last night."

"How did that go?" asked Horse.

"Actually, it didn't go very well. But, that's already old news."

"What do you mean?" I asked, wondering where he was going with this.

He grinned. "Well, today, we talked and I think we've cleared up our issues. We even called a truce."

"No shit?" said Chopper.

"That's right," he replied, smiling around at everyone. I had to give him credit, he was smooth when he wanted to be. "The shit between us is all smoothed over. We're good."

"What about Breaker?" asked Horse.

His smile faltered. "Well, as usual, my fucking temper got the best of me when I first found out about the incident. But we all know that you can't go pointing fingers without evidence. Truth is, we have no proof that Breaker is the one who attacked Jessica. Could have been a number of fuckers. Hell, she's not even sure herself who did it."

"But they were wearing a cut that matched the Devil's Rangers," said Chopper, looking frustrated. "Come one, Prez. You know one of them did it. You fucking know they did."

"I have to agree with Slammer," said Buck. "Unless we know for sure who did it, we can't go killing people without proof. Can't kill an innocent man for another man's sins."

"Yeah, but, he's the only one who's done time for rape," said Chopper.

"You know this, how?" asked Slammer.

Chopper grunted. "I'm your Intelligence Officer, come on. It didn't take me long to find this shit out."

"No, I suppose it wouldn't," he replied.

"You sure you want to let this go?" asked Horse.

"Like I said before, no proof. Plus, I gave Mud my word that none of the Gold Vipers would touch Breaker," he replied. He looked at me and then the others. "And I plan on keeping my word. There will be no retaliation. No revenge, no nothing. Understood?"

We all agreed.

Chapter Twenty-One

Adriana

Fortunately, the rest of the day was uneventful at the shop and there were no more calls from that freak, Breaker. Trevor didn't call me back, either. Nor did he show up at the store, which was kind of a relief. My mom would have flipped her lid.

When six o'clock rolled around, we locked the doors and began doing inventory. Jim stuck around, which I was grateful for, since being alone at a jewelry store at night was disconcerting. After we checked off each piece of jewelry, Jim carefully placed them into the large walk-in safe, where they'd stay until morning. By the time nine o'clock rolled around, we'd finished with all one-hundred-and ninety-two pieces, and I couldn't wait leave. Reading all the item numbers on the tiny tags was exhausting.

"There has got to be an easier way of doing inventory," I told her.

"There is, but I like doing it this way."

"But they have these scanners you can use, now, Mom. You'd keep much better track of each piece."

"It's far too expensive to set that up," she said and then smiled. "Our way is already paid for."

She was so frugal and old fashioned at times it was aggravating. "Fine. If you like doing things the hard way."

"It's easy with your help. Now, let's go to Sicily's," my mother said, as we were locking up the shop. "My treat for making you do things the hard way. You too, Jim."

"Sure, if you insist," said Jim, his eyes twinkling. "I love Italian food."

"Mom, I'm sorry, I just can't," I replied, grabbing the car keys out of my purse. "I'm meeting up with Krystal."

She stopped in her tracks. "Again? I thought you celebrated her birthday last night," she replied, frowning.

"I know. This is just us, though. Last night was crazy and we didn't get much of a chance to talk."

"Didn't you have enough time to talk when you spent the night at her house?"

"No. We crashed pretty quickly," I lied.

"I'll meet you at the restaurant," said Jim, heading toward his car. I could tell he didn't want any part of the conversation.

"Goodbye," I called.

Jim turned around and waved as he reached his Toyota. "Have a good night, Adriana," he replied and then looked at Mom. "I'll see you soon?"

"Yes," she said, smiling. "Very soon."

He smiled back and got into his car.

She turned back to me. "You're not going to meet that man on the motorcycle afterward, are you?"

"Mom, would you just give it up," I said, frustrated. "I know what I'm doing."

"No, Adriana, I don't think you do. You're only twenty-one and I'm sure bad boys like that seem sexy, but —"

"Bad boys? Mom, please," I interrupted as I began walking to my car, which was parked next to hers. "It's not like that."

"It sure looked like that way to me earlier," she said, coming up behind me. "The way you two were attacking each other in the driveway."

"It was just a couple of kisses," I said, getting into the car. "Really, you don't need to worry about me."

Her eyes softened. "I can't help it. You're my daughter."

Your *grown* daughter," I reminded her. "Look, take Jim out to dinner and enjoy yourself." I lowered my voice. "It's obvious the man is crazy about you."

She looked shocked. "What? No. No, he isn't."

I glanced back over at Jim, who was sitting in his car, waiting for her. "Oh yes, he is. You just don't see it. Quit worrying about me and think about yourself for a change. Go on a date, have some fun."

She looked over her shoulder at him and then sighed. "A date?"

"Yes. Pretend it's a date."

"I can't do that to your father's memory. I still love him and it wouldn't be right."

"Mom, you don't have to stop loving Dad," I said softly. "But don't deny yourself companionship with someone who adores you. Someone like Jim, who's nice and is always there for you."

She chewed on her lower lip. "You really think he *adores* me?"

"I guess you haven't noticed the way he looks at you. He definitely has a crush."

"A crush?" Her cheeks flushed. "Really?"

"Yes, really. Aren't you attracted to him?"

"I guess... I haven't thought about it. I mean, he's nice looking."

"Mom, seriously, you're too young to become an old spinster."

She laughed. "An old spinster?"

I smiled. "That's right. If you look up the word in the dictionary, you might find your picture there soon, if you don't do something."

Mom smirked. "You think I don't know what you're doing?"

"What do you mean?"

"Changing the subject."

"What I'm doing is letting you know that you can't control who is in my life but you can control who is in yours. Right now there's a sweet guy who is meeting you at Sicily's. He likes you. A lot. Who knows, maybe you'll find that you like him, too. And not just as your security guard."

She looked at Jim's car again but didn't say anything.

My cell phone went off.

"It's Krystal. I've gotta go," I said, looking down at it.

"Just be careful," Vanda replied, crossing her arms under her chest.

"I will, and have fun," I said, winking at her before slamming the door shut.

She turned and walked over to her car.

"Hi, Krystal," I said, answering the phone.

"Hey, guess what?" she said. There were voices in the background and I could tell she was someplace crowded.

"What?" I asked, starting my engine.

"We found him."

"Found who? *Jason?*"

"Hell yes. I'm in the bathroom now. At Club Hideaway. I found out from Gary that he was heading here tonight. Tank and Raptor are keeping an eye on Jason. I think they're going to confront the prick outside, since the place is crawling with bouncers."

My heart began to race. "Oh, my God, I'm on my way."

"Okay. I'll let you know if we leave or if something happens."

"I'm twenty minutes away. I'll get there as quickly as possible."

We hung up and I pulled out of the parking lot, wondering what they planned on doing to Jason once they had him alone. Would they just kick his ass or threaten him with a weapon?

This is crazy, I thought. *I should have just called the police. Someone is going to get hurt.*

I turned a corner and a few seconds later and I noticed the person behind me had their high-beams on. Then I noticed that it was a truck. Breaker's.

"Oh, my God," I gasped, moving quickly into the right lane. I watched in horror as he followed me. I tried zigzagging around other cars, desperate to put some distance behind us, but Breaker kept up. Frightened, I hopped onto the freeway and raced toward the club, not knowing what else to do. If anything, I could lead him to Trevor. Soon, I was going eighty miles an hour in the passing lane, thankful that it wasn't rush hour.

"Where the fuck are the cops when you need them?" I said out loud, wishing that I'd catch one of their radars. But, for some crazy reason, even though it was a Saturday night, and I was driving like a bat out of hell, they weren't around. Frustrated, I looked into the mirror and noticed that Breaker was still hot on my tail. "Dammit, you are such a freak!"

His laughter from earlier echoed in my head. I was pretty sure he was having a blast, scaring the hell out of me. I just couldn't understand why he was so obsessed with someone he'd just met.

Because he's fucking insane.

We drove like this, with me driving like a maniac and him following suit, until I noticed we were finally approaching downtown Iowa City. I put my blinker on and was about to enter the right lane to get off at the next exit, when he quickly moved into it, blocking me.

"Dammit," I yelled, slowing down.

He also slowed down and then sped up as I tried to maneuver my way into the lane. Of course, I missed the exit.

"Fuck you, asshole," I mumbled, thinking that at least he'd gotten off, and was no longer following me. But, when I looked back into the rearview mirror, I found that I was wrong. He'd obviously jumped off of the exit at the last minute, and was tailing me again.

Furious, I pressed my foot firmly on the gas and flew down the freeway, determined to stay ahead of him so I could get off on the next exit. This time it worked, and I was able to take the next ramp, with him one car behind. As I turned and then headed toward Main Street, I recalled where the local cop shop was and decided to lead him there instead of going to the club.

"You want to follow me, asshole. Go right ahead," I said, staring at him in the rearview mirror.

Just as I predicted, he continued to follow me, but then, as I reached the police station, he turned off, waving at me through his open window.

"Yeah, that's what I thought. You fucking coward," I mumbled, going the opposite direction.

***

Chapter Twenty-Two

BREAKER

"Where are you at?" barked Mud.

"Just driving around," he answered, following the brunette. He couldn't wait to get his hands on her hot little body as well as that rock around her neck. The sapphire had to be worth thirty or forty grand.

"You need to get your ass down to the clubhouse, brother. Rumor has it that 'The Judge' might be looking for your ass."

His eyes widened. "The Judge? Where'd you hear that?"

"Misty. She overheard Slammer talking about it earlier. Called and give me the heads-up."

"I'm not afraid of that asshole. I'll slice his nuts off if he tries taking me down. Shove them up his ass."

"You'd better be. From what I hear, the guy has never missed a delivery, and this time, you're the one on order. Now, get your ass back here so we can figure this shit out."

Breaker sighed. That foxy little Adriana was just going to have to wait. "I'll be there in twenty."

"Don't stop off anywhere. We'll be watching for you."

Click.

Breaker set his phone down and got into the right lane. As he was about to turn, he rolled his window down and waved at Adriana. He couldn't see her face, but something told him that she wasn't smiling. In fact, he was pretty sure he'd scared the hell out of her. The knowledge made his cock swell.

"Mother fucking Prez," he mumbled, lighting a smoke. He loved Mud and the rest of the crew, but in reality, they really were a bunch of pussies. Every last one of them. His brothers seemed to shake in their boots whenever 'The Judge' was mentioned. Well, he wasn't afraid of the Zorro-wannabe-faggot. The Judge was a joke. He wasn't even part of any club. The fact was, he would love to face the asshole and show him who the real judge was. Maybe stick a gavel up his ass and call it a night.

Laughing to himself, Breaker turned down a dark, dead-end street and parked his truck in a quiet spot. He couldn't help it – he needed to get off. Chasing Adriana had wound him up and now, all he could think about was fucking the little cunt. Pushing the 'Play' button on his stereo, he began listening to the CD he'd made. The one where he'd recorded the last bitch's screams. Jessica's. The fact that it was Slammer's Old Lady's daughter made it that much more exhilarating. He'd noticed the girl when he'd been trailing Slammer last summer. Saw her leaving his house. From that moment on, he'd followed the sweet piece of tail everywhere, waiting for the right opportunity. When he'd noticed her roommate leave with a suitcase a couple weeks back, he'd broken in and made himself at home. The rest was history. Sweet history that he'd recorded for his own sick pleasure. Sure, he knew he was a little twisted, but it didn't change the fact that he enjoyed torturing women. Making them beg for their lives.

Breaker got rid of his cigarette and unzipped his pants. Imagining himself on top of Adriana, he spit in his hand and began to jerk off.

"Yeah, baby," he whispered, moving his hand up and down as the girl on the CD whimpered, begging him to stop. He closed his eyes.

"Look at me," demanded the voice on the CD. His voice. "You see me?"

Panting, Breaker remembered the terror in Jessica's eyes as he stared into them, and it brought him to the edge. Just as he was about to blow his load, he felt the cool barrel of a gun against his temple.

Gasping, he opened his eyes and found himself staring at a man he didn't recognize.

"You're one ugly cuss, you know that? I can also see why don't get many dates," said the man, turning down the stereo. "Also, I don't know if anyone has ever told you, but your taste in music is pretty fucked up."

"Who the hell are you?" he said, trying to shove his dick back into his jeans.

He smirked. "If you have to ask, you're even dumber than I thought."

"Fuck you," he growled.

"Why don't you beg? Like the girl on the CD, you sick fuck…"

"Go to hell."

"Thanks for the invite, but I'm not ready yet. Tell everyone that I said hello."

Breaker's face turned white. "Wait a minute. I've got money, too. I'll pay you double. Whatever they offered, I'll pay more."

"This one isn't about the money." He lowered the gun to Breaker's limp dick. "It's about a girl whose life you ruined," he said, pulling the trigger.

Chapter Twenty-Three

Adriana

I pulled into a parking lot, which was across the street from Club Hideaway, and parked the car. Then I texted Krystal. She called me right away.

"Perfect timing. The shit is about to hit the fan. Jason is heading toward the door with some girl, and we're getting ready to follow him."

"I'll wait out here. I don't want him to see me."

"Good idea. I'll call you right back," she said, hanging up.

I stayed in my car and watched the front door, anxious and scared at the same time. A few minutes later, I saw Jason step outside with a girl. He had his arm around her shoulders. I noticed she was lucid and actually seemed to be enjoying their conversation. It made me wonder if I was wrong about everything. Sure, he'd been an asshole, but had he really drugged me?

As they walked toward the parking lot where I was hunched in my car, the club doors opened again. This time, Trevor, Tank, and Krystal stepped outside.

Blowing out my breath, I watched as the three kept their distance and followed them into the parking lot. Just as Jason approached his car, which was a couple rows away from mine, Trevor confronted him.

***

Raptor

"Excuse me, Jason?"

He turned around and looked at me.

"I'm sorry, do I know you?" he asked.

"No, but I think you know her," said Tank, nodding to Krystal.

Jason's face turned pale. "Ah, hey, Krystal. What's going on?"

Krystal smiled coldly. "Heard you abandoned my friend last night. After you tried raping her, you fucking asshole."

The girl standing next to Jason took a step back. "What? Jason, what is she talking about?"

"Nothing, Michelle. Get in the car. I'll handle this."

"But –"

"Get in the car," he said firmly. "Please."

Sighing, she opened the door and slid into the front seat.

Jason turned back to us. "What's this all about?"

"You slipped something into Adriana's drink last night," I said. "What was it?"

His face darkened. "That's bullshit. I didn't do any such thing. Is that what she told you?"

In three strides I had him by the throat. "Look, you ass-fuck," I spat. "That shit could have killed her. What the fuck was it?"

He tried clawing at my fingers. "I didn't," he croaked. "Let me go."

I reached into my jacket and pulled out my revolver. I held it to his head and cocked it. "Tell me or I'll blow your head off, motherfucker."

"Oh, my God, no!" hollered Adriana, who was running toward us. "Don't!"

I lowered the gun and shoved it into his nut-sack. "Don't worry, Jason. I'm not going to kill you. Just remove the source of your problem."

"Please," he begged, holding up his hands. "It wasn't me. Seriously. It was Lucas. He did it. For Gary. It was his birthday."

I glared at him. "Explain."

"Lucas just wanted him to get lucky. The shit was just supposed to make her horny. That's all I know."

"Gary wasn't interested in having sex with any of us," said Krystal, looking horrified. "Don't put the blame on him."

"I'm not. I mean, you're right. He didn't even know about it."

"But you did," I said sharply. "And you tried raping her."

"No," he lied. "I swear…"

"Say goodbye to your little friends," I said, mimicking Al Pacino.

He began to cry. "No! Please! I'll do anything."

I heard the sound of sirens in the distance.

"Time to leave," said Tank.

Swearing, I slammed my fist into Jason's face and heard the distinct sound of his nose breaking.

He sank to his knees holding his nose. "I think you broke it. Oh, my God!"

I grinned. "Good. It looks like it's your lucky day, fuck-face, because that's all I have time for. Now, I know you've heard of the Gold Vipers and now we've heard of you."

Jason's eyes moved to my jacket and the realization of who I was associated with made him look like he was going to shit his pants.

I grabbed him by the collar and looked down into his face. "I ever hear of you or your friends drugging these or any other girls, you're dead. You feel me?"

He nodded quickly.

"I mean it. You'll be ten feet under and I'll bury you myself if I have to. I have plenty of shovels."

"I won't. I swear," he cried.

Although I still wanted to beat the fuck out of Jason, I released him.

"Let's bolt. The cops are getting close," said Tank.

I turned toward Adriana, but she wouldn't even look at me. Sighing, I grabbed her by the elbow and began ushering her to the car she'd gotten out of. "Meet me at my house," I said, when we stopped.

"No," she said, pulling her arm away. She continued to avoid my eyes. "I can't."

"I'm coming with you, Adriana," said Krystal, approaching the car.

"Okay," she answered.

"We need to talk," I said, feeling the tension between us. I couldn't understand why she was pissed. The guy got off with a broken nose. Shit could have been a lot worse.

She didn't say anything, but I could tell the wheels in her head were turning rapidly.

"Raptor," said Tank. "I'll meet you back by the bikes."

"I'm right behind you, brother."

Tank held up his hand. "Call me, Krystal."

She nodded. "Yeah. I will."

"So, you have a gun," blurted out Adriana, looking angry.

"Yeah, so?"

"Yeah, *so?*" she said, laughing coldly. "I guess my mother was right. You're not just trouble, you are fucking dangerous."

I tried to remain calm, but it wasn't easy. My adrenaline was still on overdrive. "Not to you."

"Famous last words."

"Bullshit. I would never hurt you," I said, staring at her in frustration.

"You've got that right. Goodbye, Trevor," said Adriana, getting into her car.

I wanted to stop her, but I could see the cherries from the cops heading down the street. Swearing, I took off running.

Chapter Twenty-Four

Adriana

"Wasn't that insane?" said Krystal, digging around in her purse.

"Very."

"God, I need a cigarette."

"I thought you were quitting."

"I was, but after that scene, can you blame me?"

I smiled grimly. "No. I guess not."

"Do you have some cash on you?" she asked, pulling out her wallet. "All I have is a five dollar bill and I've already maxed my credit card."

"Another reason why you should quit smoking."

"Don't be a drag," she said, laughing.

I rolled my eyes.

"Seriously, can you loan me a couple bucks for a pack of smokes?"

"Yeah, fine."

"Thanks."

"Where's your car?"

"At their clubhouse."

"Where is that?"

"A couple blocks away from Griffin's."

"You want me to drop you off there, right?"

"If you could?"

"Why not? I've got nothing else going on."

She sucked in a breath. "Is that the necklace from your dad?" she asked, leaning toward me.

I touched it and smiled. "Yeah."

"I can't believe you're wearing it. It's beautiful."

"Thanks. I have to admit, I was nervous wearing the thing."

"I would be, too. If someone found out it was real, they'd try and steal it."

"Speaking of which…" I told her about Breaker, from when I first ran into him, at the gas station, to where he chased me after work.

She stared at me in horror. "Oh, my God, are you serious?!"

"Yeah. It was scary. I headed toward the police station and he must have known what I was doing, because that's when he left me."

"That prick. You should call Raptor and let him know."

I shook my head. "Oh, no. I don't want *anything* to do with him."

"You know, he has the hots for you."

"I don't care. Raptor is fucking crazy," I said firmly. "You saw him back there. He could have shot Jason."

"Why do you care? The guy is a douchebag."

I looked at her in surprise. "Don't tell me you're condoning murder now?"

"No, of course not. But, Raptor was just trying to scare him. Now he'll think twice about drugging girls for sex."

"After that, you'd think so."

We pulled into a nearby gas station. She ran inside and bought a pack of smokes. When she got back into the car, she asked me if she could light one up.

I grunted. "Seriously? I just bought it. It still smells new."

"What if I open the window?"

I frowned. "You know that doesn't really help."

"Fine," she pouted, shoving the cigarettes into her purse.

I let out an exasperated sigh. "Do you want me to pull over somewhere so you can have one?"

"No. I'll just wait until we get to my car," she said, looking out her side window. She was silent for several minutes and I knew something was definitely wrong.

"You mad?" I asked.

"No," she replied, looking back at me. "I'm just thinking about Tank. I'm afraid of what he's going to do when I break it off with him."

"So, you're really going to do it?"

She nodded.

"Good. They're both bad news. I'm sure Tank carries a gun, too."

"He does."

"Great. Well, if I were you, I would definitely do it over the phone."

She smirked. "I was planning on it."

"So, where is this place?" I asked, as we neared Griffin's.

She directed me past the strip joint to a warehouse district, about two miles away. We pulled up to a set of gates.

"Great, how do we get in there?"

"Very easily. It's not locked," she said, opening the car door. "I'll be right back."

"Okay."

Krystal got out and ran up to the gate. She unlatched it and pulled it open. I drove through it and waited for her to get back in.

"My car is just over there," she said, pointing to a row of vehicles that were parked near the side of an old warehouse.

"So, this is where these guys usually hang out, huh?" I said, driving slowly. "The building looks abandoned, except for the cars."

"Most of those belong to the club whores," she said, wrinkling her nose. "The guys keep their bikes inside of the building. There's a garage door in back."

"Why are the windows all boarded up?" I asked, stopping behind her car.

"Because of the shit that goes on inside," she said, picking up her purse. "It's like a playground for men in there. They've got this wraparound bar with hundreds of bottles of booze. *Hundreds*. A couple of wide screen TVs, some video and pinball machines." She smirked. "Hell, they even have a stripper pole."

"Why does that not surprise me?"

"I know, right? Get this, some of the girls walk around naked, like it's no big deal."

"Classy."

"Exactly. Anyway, I'd better go," she leaned over and gave me a hug. "I'm just going to go home and crash, I think. I'm still a little hung over from last night. I tried the old 'Hair-of-the-dog' thing, but it's not working."

"Okay. Call me, tomorrow."

"I will."

Krystal got out and walked over to her car. As I watched her get inside, my cell phone went off.

Trevor.

I ignored his call but then he began texting me. Sighing, I picked up my phone and called him.

"Where are you?" he asked.

"I just dropped Krystal off to her car and now I'm on my way home," I replied, backing out of the parking lot.

"Wait there for me. I want to talk to you. I'm only a couple minutes away."

"We have nothing to talk about."

"Yes. We do."

"Look, I'm grateful for what you did, picking me up in the middle of the night and letting me stay at your house, but it can't go any further than that."

"That's not what I got from that kiss, earlier."

That was before I saw you almost kill someone.

"Things have changed," I said, driving away from the clubhouse. Knowing that he was almost there, I wanted to put as much distance between him and my car as I could.

"What do you mean?"

"I think you know exactly what I mean. That thing with Jason..."

"He needed to be taught a lesson."

"You broke his nose."

"Yes, I did."

"And you threatened him with a gun."

"Of course I did. He needed to know we meant business."

I sighed.

"Did you expect me to ask him nicely?"

"No, but I didn't expect that!"

"Look, Kitten, he deserved a lot more than what I dished out, believe me."

"He wasn't even the one who slipped me the drug."

"No, but he knew about it and tried to use it to his advantage, didn't he?"

"Yes, but –"

"And then he threw you out of his car, in the middle of nowhere, without giving a shit. You're probably lucky to be alive. Are you really going to stick up for that asshole?"

He had a point.

"No. I'm not. I just don't like the way you handled the situation."

"I did what I had to do, to 'handle it'. And because I scared the fuck out of him, College Boy will think twice before trying something like that again. I guarantee it."

"I'd say."

"Now, if that's all you're pissed at, then I need to see you, Kitten. Tonight. Are we good?"

"I… um…I guess so. I'm kind of tired. Maybe we could have lunch or something, tomorrow?"

"Lunch?"

"Yeah."

He chuckled. "Hell, we can do that, too. I'll see you soon."

"But –"

"Meet me at my place." He hung up.

I stared at the phone and realized this was the second time, in twenty-four hours, that he'd cut me off when I'd tried to say 'No'. He obviously didn't do well with that word.

Sighing, I put my phone down and headed toward my own house. If he wasn't going to listen to my protests, he'd sure as hell hear my actions loud and clear.

Chapter Twenty-Five

Adriana

When I arrived home, I sent Trevor a text, telling him that I wasn't coming over. In the message I also explained that I wasn't interested in seeing him again, because his world frightened the hell out of me. I also told him that if he called, I wouldn't answer. I pretty much demanded that he give me space and respect my wishes.

I hesitated before I pushed "Send." I hesitated, because deep down, part of me wanted to see that sexy smile again. Even more than that, I wanted him to kiss me. I wanted his tongue, his mouth, and what was hiding under those blue jeans. I wanted it badly. What I didn't want was the drama and all of the other stuff that came with it. Something told me that if I did find myself in his bed, I'd make up excuses for that part of his life. It would suddenly be, acceptable. Well, that was now unacceptable.

Letting out a ragged breath, I pushed "Send" and then waited several minutes for his reaction.

Fortunately, he didn't call me back.

Nor did he send me a text.

Setting my phone down, I went into my bedroom, removed my pantyhose, and then threw them into the dirty clothes. Afterward, I went into the kitchen and began making myself a ham and cheese sandwich. As I was searching for the mayonnaise, I heard it. The rumble of a motorcycle rolling down the street.

Groaning, I closed the refrigerator and went to the front door, knowing that none of the other neighbors owned a Harley or any other motorcycle for that matter. When I opened it, I found myself looking up at Trevor's cocky grin.

"Surprise."

I scowled. "Didn't you get my text?"

"Of course."

"I told you not to come over here."

"Number one, you should know that I'm not keen on following orders, unless they're from Slammer. Number two, you told me not to *call* you. You never said anything about stopping by."

I sighed. "Technicalities."

"Can I come in?"

"No," I said, crossing my arms under my chest. "In fact, you really need to leave. My mother is going to be home soon."

"So, what you're really trying to say is that she doesn't like me?"

"Ha, ha. Funny."

"Actually, it's not, really." He looked down at my outfit and he whistled. "I didn't get a chance to tell you this, but you look sexier than hell, Kitten."

"Thanks."

He bit his lower lip and sighed. "A dress like that can make a man lose control. It can also put ideas in his head. Wicked ones."

I was blushing when our eyes met again.

"Come on." He leaned against the doorframe and whispered, "Take a ride with me."

"I can't."

"You can. You're just scared."

"It would never work between us."

"I'm not asking for anything to work. I'm just asking you to take a ride."

I glanced at his Harley. It sounded like fun, but I knew it was a bad idea. Between the man and the machine, I'd never want to get off. Or maybe I would and that was the real problem. "What do you want from me, Trevor?"

A slow, sexy smile crossed his lips. "Oh, darling, do you really have to ask?"

Why the fuck did he have to be so damn sexy?

"If I get on your bike, I'm pretty sure I'll make some bad decisions before the night is over."

He grinned wickedly. "I won't tell if you won't."

Heat pooled between my legs. The look in his eyes was making it so hard. "I'm not getting on your bike, so don't ask me again."

He sighed. "Fine. I won't ask you again if you agree to something."

"What's that?"

"Give me a kiss goodbye. You owe me, anyway."

I laughed. "Oh, is that right?"

He looked serious. "Yeah. It's colder than shit out here and now I have to drive back."

"Why is that my problem?"

"Because you wouldn't let me call you. Had I been able to do so, I wouldn't be standing out here or about to drive back without your warm body wrapped around me on my bike."

"So, you think I owe you a kiss?" I replied, smirking.

"Probably two, but I'll settle for one."

I smirked. "Fine. One kiss and then you're leaving."

He stepped closer to me and slid his arms around my waist. "I swear I'll leave, if you still want me to," he whispered, staring down at my mouth.

Bad mistake, I thought, feeling my body already begin to respond. Just the feel of his arms around me was making my stomach quiver.

"I'm sure I will," I lied, more to myself than him.

He smiled and then leaned forward, kissing me gently. I closed my eyes, feeling a surge of excitement as his tongue slid into my mouth. His mouth was hot and he tasted like spearmint and beer, it was an oddly seductive mix. I slid my hand up to the back of his neck and began kissing him back, wanting more. Needing more. The man was as bad as a drug. The addicting kind.

Trevor growled in the back of his throat and pulled away. "Take a ride with me," he said, sliding his hands over my ass. He pressed his hips against mine and I could feel his hardness, teasing me. "Please. I've got to have you."

"I… I can't," I whispered, his words making me wetter than the birdbath out front.

"You can," he murmured, moving his lips to my neck. "Fuck me, you smell good."

"The neighbors are watching," I whispered, noting that the woman across the street was looking through her blinds.

"Oh, yeah? Well, this show is all mine," he whispered, backing me into the house. When my shoulders hit the closet door, he pulled me back against his chest and began kissing me again, this time much more hungrily. Then one of his hands was on my breast, the other on my ass. He started squeezing both, while grinding his hips into mine, letting me know what his intentions were.

I moaned, kissing him back as he raised my dress and touched my thong.

"Fuck, you're killing me," he growled, slamming the door shut with the back of his boot. "I need to be inside of you. Now."

"What are you doing?" I squealed, as he picked me up.

His blue eyes burned into mine. His pupils were large. "Where's your bedroom?"

"Upstairs, but we can't. My mother will be home soon."

"This is your house, too?"

"Yes."

"Are you an adult?"

"Yes."

"Then let's go act like adults," he said, heading toward the stairs. Seconds later, we were in my bedroom and he was locking the door.

"I... I don't think this is a good idea," I said.

He turned around and began removing his leather jacket. "Let me do the thinking."

I smiled nervously.

He hung his jacket on my door and glanced around the room. It was still painted purple and I had the same frilly bedspread covering my mattress I'd had when I was a teenager.

He chuckled.

"What?"

"The only thing missing are posters of boy-bands and puppies. You certainly have enough stuffed animals and... unicorns."

"I used to collect them," I said, glancing at all the figurines.

He removed his leather cut and hung it over the jacket. Then he pulled his T-shirt out of his jeans and began taking it off. "I used to collect rocks and crystals before my old man threw them out one day. Then I just didn't bother with it anymore. Nothing wrong with wanting to collect things."

"I agree," I replied, staring at his tattooed, muscular chest and arms. "And, I think that's great. Collecting rocks and crystals."

He walked over to me and touched my necklace. "Speaking of," said Trevor. "I want to see you naked, wearing this and nothing else," he said, his eyes burning into mine.

I looked down at it, my cheeks burning red.

"Fuck, you're beautiful. Come here." He grabbed the back of my head, and pulled my face to his, kissing me hard.

I melted into Trevor, the very last of my resolve, gone. I couldn't wait to feel his cock moving deep inside of me. Just the thought of it made my sex tighten up.

His kisses became more demanding as my hand moved to the hard bulge hidden in his jeans. As I began stroking him, his tongue plunged deep, filling my mouth the way we both wanted him to fill my sex.

"I'm going to explode, I want you so fucking bad, Kitten," he growled into my neck as I squeezed his cock through his jeans. I could feel the long, hard, length of him through the denim and it made me want to hump his leg like a bitch in heat.

Panting, he pulled my dress up and over my hips, then slid his hand to the front of my thong where he cupped my mound. "Fuck," he whispered, using his knuckles to stroke my clit through the fabric. "I need to be inside of you. You want me to fuck you?"

"Yes," I moaned, digging my nails into his arm. "Oh God, yes."

He slid one of his fingers into me. "You're so wet."

Whimpering in pleasure I unbuttoned his jeans and slid my hand under his boxers, grappling his cock. The size alone almost brought me to my knees. I couldn't wait to ride him.

Gasping, he grabbed my wrist as I began stroking him. "Hold on, there, darlin'. I won't last."

I smiled.

He kicked his jeans and boxers down to the floor, his cock bobbing as he pushed them aside with his foot. I could almost taste the pre-cum dripping on the end and it made me even more wet.

***

Raptor

My dick was so hard that two more strokes would have done me in. I made her stop and got rid of my jeans. Then I walked over to the bed and sat down on the edge. "Undress for me," I said, staring up at her.

Her cheeks turned pink.

I grinned. "Come on, Kitten. Don't be shy. Turn around."

She did and I unzipped her dress. It fell to the floor and she kicked it away. As she was about to turn back around, I stopped her.

"Hold on. I need to look at this pretty little ass of yours," I said, grabbing it with both hands.

She squealed as I leaned forward and bit her left cheek, playfully.

"That hurts," she said, trying to move away.

"Let me kiss it then," I said, bringing my mouth back to her creamy skin. I licked where it was pink and she began to relax.

"You've got a sweet ass," I said, moving a finger down the length of her thong to her slit, which was dripping wet.

She moaned.

I licked my lips. "Spread your legs more."

Adriana, did as she was told.

I shoved my thumb into her hole as I circled and wiggled around on her clit with my other two fingers. Moaning, she leaned forward, holding her knees and I couldn't take it anymore. I needed a taste of that that peach. I turned her around, picked her up, and sat her on my face.

"Oh, my God," she gasped as I slid her G-string to the side and began licking her pussy.

"Ah... ah..."

I stopped and looked up at her. "Is this okay?"

Adriana stared at me through her lashes. "Yes," she murmured, her face flushed. "Very."

Grabbing her hips, I plunged my tongue, deep into her hole, tickling her clit with my nose. Moaning, she leaned forward and grabbed the headboard to steady herself as I licked and sucked in the places that I knew drove women crazy.

"Yes," whimpered, as my tongue moved faster. "Oh, my God, Trevor…"

Noticing that she still had her bra on, I paused, sliding my hand up to her breasts. I tugged at it. "Take this off."

I could feel her legs trembling as she unclasped her bra and threw it aside.

"Beautiful," I whispered.

She had perfect breasts. Not too big. Not too small. Plus, they were real. Unlike Brandy's.

Staring up at her gorgeous body, I continued to work her clit with my tongue, while I stared up at her breasts. Reaching up, I grabbed one, enjoying the softness and weight in my palm. I squeezed it and then my hand went to the other, this time pinching her nipple. Moaning, she leaned back and grabbed my cock, stroking it.

Resisting the urge to let her keep pumping my cock, I stopped her and flipped us over.

****

Adriana

Trevor got back between my legs and began licking my clit again. His rhythm was steady, as he followed up with his fingers inside of my sex. He kept a slow, steady pressure, rubbing back and forth while continually teasing me with his expert tongue. I began to squirm, feeling my orgasm build.

"Yes," I whimpered. "Keep doing that."

Staring up at me with hooded eyes, he began to put extra pressure on my clit, his tongue more demanding and his fingers knowing exactly where I needed them. It didn't take long before it all got to me and I was crying out, my hips convulsing as I came.

"Mm... Kitten, you're so sexy," Trevor whispered, licking me as the tremors subsided. "I can't wait to get inside of –"

The sound of the doorbell shocked us both.

"Oh, my God," I said, jumping out of bed. "Ignore it."

My heart was pounding a mile a minute. I felt like a teenager who was about to get caught doing something bad. "What if it's my mother? She could be locked out of the house."

He sighed. "Doesn't she have a spare key?"

"Yes, probably," I said, peeking out my bedroom window. What I saw parked in front of my house made my heart actually stop.

"Can you see anything?"

I backed away from the window and headed to my dresser. "There's an unmarked police car here," I said, grabbing a pair of sweats and a T-shirt. I looked at him. "Do you think they're here because of Jason?"

"Probably," he said, grabbing his jeans. "I'm sorry. I didn't want to get you into trouble. I guess I fucked that this up pretty badly. I didn't think he'd talk."

"He almost raped me," I said, pulling up the sweats. "If anyone should be in trouble, it should be him. Wait up here. I'll tell them that I don't know you."

"No, I'll come with you. I'm not going to hide."

The doorbell rang again.

"It's easier this way," I said, pulling my T-shirt over my head as I walked out of my bedroom. I ran down the steps and opened the door. There were two cops, a male and a female.

"Can I help you?"

"Are you Adriana Nikolas?" asked the woman, her expression grim.

"Yes."

She showed me her badge. "I'm Detective Tabitha Williams, and this is my partner, Jeremy Stone. We'd like to come in and ask you a few questions."

"About what?"

"Your friend, Krystal Blake."

I stared at her in confusion. "Krystal? I don't understand. Why are you here asking about her?"

"She's missing."

Chapter Twenty-Six

Adriana

"Missing," I repeated, the blood rushing to my head. "What do you mean, *missing*? I just left her about two hours ago."

"That's what we'd like to talk to you about, Ms. Nikolas," answered Detective Stone. He turned and nodded toward Trevor's bike. "Whose motorcycle is that in your driveway?"

"It's mine," said Trevor, coming up behind me. He put his arm around my shoulder. "Can you tell us what's going on?"

"And you are?" asked Detective Williams.

"He's a friend," I answered quickly. "Look, you said Krystal was missing. What exactly do you mean by that? I just left her about an hour ago."

"Let's go inside and we'll talk about it," replied Detective Williams.

"Fine," I said, moving back to let them in.

The two detectives followed us into the living room and we all sat down.

"I spoke to Krystal's mother and she mentioned that you were meeting her this evening?" asked Detective Stone.

"Yes. I met her at Club Hideaway and then shortly afterwards I gave her a ride to her car."

"You dropped her off at her car?" asked the woman. "Where was that?"

Trevor actually gave them the address but it was obvious the detectives both knew where her car had been parked.

"That's where you and your gang hang out, isn't it?" asked Detective Williams, nodding toward Trevor's cut. "The Gold Vipers?"

"It's our clubhouse."

"Excuse me, what did you say your name was?" she asked, pulling out a small notepad.

"I didn't. It's Raptor," he replied.

"Raptor?" She stared at him, a cool smile on her face. "Could you give us your birth name? That would make things so much easier."

"Sure. It's Trevor Larson."

She wrote it down. "And, what is your relationship with Ms. Nikolas?"

"Why does it matter?" he asked, frowning.

"We're investigating a woman's disappearance, Mr. Larson. We need to know as much we can about Krystal and the people in her life, to help in this investigation. Obviously, Ms. Nikolas and Krystal are friends. I imagine," she looked at my hair, "that you and Ms. Nikolas are lovers?"

Embarrassed, I touched my hair, which felt like it was in total disarray. I could only imagine my appearance after what had just happened upstairs.

"We're halfway there," replied Trevor with a straight face.

My cheeks turned scarlet.

Detective Williams smirked. "Well, we apologize for interrupting your plans for the evening. We only have a few questions for you and then you can get back to whatever it was you were doing."

"Right. I doubt will be doing anything after this news," said Trevor, looking at me. "We need to find her."

"Understandable. Now, have you met Krystal before, Mr. Larson?" she asked.

"Yes," he said. "I'm tight with Krystal's old man. He's my brother."

"Your brother, as in your *club* brother?" she asked.

"We may not be blood related, but he's my brother in every important sense. I'd take a fucking knife for him," he replied.

"I'm sure you would," she said, her smile fake. "And he'd probably do the same for you, I take it?"

"I would hope so," said Trevor, studying her. "Kind of like you two, right? You'd take a bullet for your partner?"

The two detectives looked at each other, but didn't comment.

"Who reported Krystal missing?" I asked, losing my patience.

"We'll get to that," said Detective Stone, clearing his throat. "First off, Ms. Nikolas, could you tell us what happened when you dropped her off at her car?"

I explained how we opened the gate and went on to tell them how I'd watched Krystal get in and start her car. "Then, I left."

"So, you left right away?" he asked.

"Yes."

He brushed a piece of lint from his slacks and then looked at me again. "Did you see anyone else in the parking lot?"

"No," I said, feeling my chest tighten. *Had someone been hiding in the parking lot?* "You said she was missing. Has she been *abducted?*"

"That's what we're trying to find out," replied Detective Williams.

I looked at Trevor. "Oh, my God," I said, feeling my eyes fill with tears. "She's my best friend. I don't know what I'd do if something happened to her," I said, trying not to cry.

He grabbed my hand. "I'm sure Krystal will be fine. If they don't find her, we will." He looked at Detective Stone. "Have you spoken to Tank?"

"Her boyfriend?" he said. "Yes. He said he doesn't know anything."

"I still don't understand what's going on," I said, sniffling. I leaned over and grabbed a tissue from the coffee table. "When I left her, she was in her car and ready to leave. Could she have driven to someone's house? Maybe she's just hanging out somewhere. In fact, I'll try calling her now," I said, standing up.

"Her car is still at the clubhouse," said Detective Stone. "So is her purse and her cell phone.

The keys were in the ignition and the car was running when we arrived at the scene."

"But she wasn't there?" I asked, sitting back down.

"No. The driver's side door was open and," Detective Stone looked at his partner and then back at me, "it looks like she lost one of her shoes."

I stared at him in horror. This was definitely foul play. There was no doubt in my mind. "Oh God, you have to find her," I said, now crying. "Please!"

Trevor put his arm around me. "She'll be found, babe. I swear, we'll find her."

"Hopefully one of us will find her in the next twenty-four hours," said Detective Stone. "That's why we need to ask you some more questions."

"How did you hear about this?" asked Trevor. "That she was missing? Did one of my crew call you?"

"We're not sure who called in the tip," said Detective Williams. "All we know is that it was a woman."

"What did she say?" asked Trevor. "Did the caller see who did it?"

"She wasn't sure, it was pretty dark, except for one streetlight. She said she was driving by the clubhouse and noticed a woman getting dragged into a van by two men, both wearing masks," said Detective Williams. "The caller became frightened when one of the men noticed her vehicle, so she sped off."

"Did she say if they wearing cuts or jackets with club patches?" asked Trevor.

"She didn't say and unfortunately, we haven't been able to trace her call," said Detective Stone.

"I need to call Slammer or Tank. See if they know what's going on," said Trevor, more to himself.

"We've spoken to Tank and his father. We also spoke to everyone who was inside your clubhouse at the time. Nobody seems to know anything," said the woman, looking frustrated. "Which, I guess would make sense since the windows are boarded up and nobody can see in or out."

"Believe me, if Tank or any of my brothers would have seen this shit go down, the fuckers would be caught by now," said Trevor.

"I don't get it," I said, looking at all of them. "Why would two men in a van kidnap her? Especially wearing masks? It's like it was planned or something."

"It almost looks that way, doesn't it?" replied Detective Stone, a strange smile on his face.

"What I don't get is why *her*," I said, dabbing at my tears. "They didn't know what time we'd be getting back to the clubhouse. Unless they were following me back there." I suddenly thought of Breaker. "Oh, my God!"

"What is it?" asked Trevor.

"That guy who has been harassing me, Breaker! He was following me again tonight. Maybe he had something to do with it!"

"Who is Breaker and why do you think he was following you?" asked the woman, sitting up straighter.

"He's a sack of shit," said Trevor, looking angry. "Who has the hots for Adriana. He followed you *again*?"

I nodded.

"I'm going to kick the shit out of him when I see the fucker," he growled.

"Now, now, Mr. Larson. Violence only leads to more trouble. If this guy is harassing her, she needs to get the law involved," said Detective Stone.

He stood up and began to pace. "The 'law' won't protect her from a bastard like Breaker. He's already been convicted of rape and I'm not going to wait for him to try and do it again, just so we can get a fucking restraining order."

"Settle down, Mr. Larson. If we're lucky, we'll link him to Ms. Blake's disappearance and that will be the end of him harassing Ms. Nikolas."

He stopped and looked at me. "It's going to be the end, no matter what, Kitten. I won't let him scare you again."

I nodded.

"Look, I'm going to ignore that threat because you haven't yet broken the law. But, I do want to remind you that should you attack this person, you could be the one going to jail," said Stone.

"I understand," said Trevor, sitting back down next to me. "And you have to understand what kind of guy we're dealing with."

"Tell us about him," said Williams.

"His real name is Thomas Kramer," said Trevor. "He's in the Devil's Rangers."

The two detectives looked at each other and then back toward us.

"This is interesting news," said Stone. "Since a man named Thomas Kramer was found dead about three hours ago."

My jaw dropped. "What?"

"He was shot and killed in his truck. What time did you say that he was following you?" asked Williams.

I told her. "It was right before I drove to Club Hideaway. I was going to make him follow me to the police station, but he turned at the last minute. I think he must have known where I was headed and changed his mind."

"Do you own a gun, Ms. Nikolas?" asked Detective Stone.

My eyes widened. "What? No!"

"Of course she doesn't own a gun," said Trevor, looking pissed off.

"How about you, Mr. Larson. Do you own a gun?" he asked him.

"Yes," replied Trevor. "I also have a Carry-And-Conceal Permit."

"What kind of gun do you own, Mr. Larson?" he asked.

"A Smith & Wesson, Thirty-Eight Special."

"Where is your gun at the moment?" asked Detective Williams, putting a hand on her holster.

"As you can see, I'm unarmed," said Trevor, holding out his arms. "And, I'm not a murderer, so you can relax."

"We're not accusing you of that." She looked at me. "I'm sorry, but we're going to have to bring you in for further questioning."

"What do you mean?" I cried, standing up. "I haven't done anything wrong."

"There's been a murder and a kidnapping tonight. You were the last person in contact with both victims, Ms. Nikolas. We need to interview you properly."

Frightened, I looked at Trevor. "Is this where I say 'Not without my lawyer present?'"

Chapter Twenty-Seven

Adriana

"Do you have something to hide, Ms. Nikolas? Because when someone brings up their lawyer, it usually means they do," said Stone, frowning.

"I've got nothing to hide," I said, glaring at him. "And I don't appreciate you making me feel like a victim."

"A victim?" he repeated.

"Yes!" I cried. "Not only have I just found out that my best friend was kidnapped, but I had this monster following me around earlier, a man who scared the hell out of me on purpose. Now, you're looking at me like I'm the guilty one around here? That's a bunch of crap!"

Just then, the front door opened and my mother walked in.

"What is going on in here?" she asked, staring at all of us in surprise.

"Mom, Krystal's been kidnapped," I said, rushing over to her.

"Kidnapped?" she repeated, as I threw my arms around her. "By whom?"

"We don't know," I said.

She patted me on the back. "Honey, I'm so sorry. That poor girl. Her mother must be worried sick."

"I haven't talked to her yet, but I'm sure she is."

"Ma'am, my name is Detective Stone and this is Detective Williams. Your daughter has agreed to come down to the precinct for an interview. You're welcome to join her."

"Of course," she said as I released her. "But, I don't understand, why does she need to do this?"

I explained what had happened, starting off with Breaker following me this morning.

"That's why you were acting so strange today," she said, looking upset. "This man was harassing you? The man that's been killed?"

I nodded. "Yes and they think I might have had something to do with it."

Her face turned red. "Of course you didn't," she said angrily. She looked at the couple. "My daughter wouldn't hurt anyone! This monster was obviously shot by someone else. How dare you even accuse her of something like this!"

"We aren't accusing her," said Stone. "We just need to interview her properly."

"Why can't you do it here?" she asked. "Adriana isn't under arrest, is she?"

"No, not at all. We'd just like to record the interview," he replied. "And see if your daughter might agree to a polygraph test."

"I can't believe this is happening," I moaned, staring at Trevor, who was very quiet.

"I'm going to call our lawyer," said Vanda, taking out her cell phone. "Before you start agreeing to anything, Adriana."

"If she's innocent, she doesn't need a lawyer," said Williams. She looked at me and sighed. "Look, just come down, pass the test, give us a statement, and you'll be on your way. That will be cheaper and a lot easier than bringing in a lawyer."

I sighed. "She's right," I said, looking at my mother. "I'm innocent. I haven't done anything wrong. I'll take the test and give them a recorded statement. If it will get them off my back."

"Are you sure?" she asked, looking concerned. "I can call him. You remember Stanley Bruebaker, don't you? He's the lawyer I used when your father passed away. I'm sure he can direct me to a lawyer that will help us with something like this."

"No, I don't remember him," I said. "Anyway, Mom, I haven't done anything wrong so it would be silly for us to fork out money when we don't need to."

"Adriana, I'm sure you haven't committed any crimes, either," said Williams, digging into her wallet. "This is really just nothing more than a formality. Here's my card with the address to the precinct. We'll meet you there?"

I nodded.

She turned to look at Trevor. "I'd like you down there, too. For further questioning."

"I'll be there," he said, moving to my side. He put his arm around my shoulders. "Now, who's going to be searching for Krystal while you waste your time with us?"

"Don't worry, Mr. Larson, we have people searching for her," she replied, smiling coolly.

"Tell me, Raptor, isn't it? Do you think Krystal's disappearance could have anything to do with Thomas Kramer's execution?" asked Detective Stone.

"Execution?" repeated Trevor. "Hmm… I don't see it."

"You don't think it might have been for some kind of retaliation between the two of your…clubs?" he asked.

Trevor's expression was stoic. "No. We're all good."

"Even with Mr. Kramer harassing your girlfriend?" asked Detective Williams.

He grunted. "Breaker deserved an ass kicking for that. But murder? That's extreme, even for us."

"Well, someone sure felt he deserved it," she replied, studying his face closely.

"I'm not saying he didn't deserve it," said Trevor. "He was the scum of the earth. A guy who enjoyed raping women. Now, some of those women he assaulted can sleep better at night."

"That was the monster who was following you today, Adriana?" asked Vanda, her eyes wide. "A convicted rapist?"

I nodded.

Her eyes were stormy as she turned to the detectives. "When you actually do find out who killed him, call me. I want to thank him personally."

"For murder?" asked Detective Williams.

"For protecting my daughter and every other girl who caught his eye," she replied.

Chapter Twenty-Eight

Raptor

When the two detectives left, Vanda turned to me. "This is your fault," she said, angrily. "If it wasn't for you, none of this would have happened."

Before I could respond, Adriana got between us. "Mom! It's not his fault. He had nothing to do with this."

"They're both in gangs," she said, waving her hand at my cut. "Obviously, they hung around each other. Didn't I tell you if you hung around biker scum that you're just looking for trouble?"

"Wait a second," I said, now glaring back at her. "You have no right to judge me or any of my crew for that matter, and I think you owe me an apology."

She snorted. "An apology? Right. What are you even doing in my house?" she said and then looked at Adriana. "Adriana, what's he doing here? Didn't we talk about this earlier? You promised you weren't going to see him again."

Clenching my jaw, I found myself hoping for the first time ever that a woman I was interested would grow a set of balls.

"I never said that," she replied. "And he had nothing to do with this. I met him through Krystal…"

"Who's been kidnapped, God forbid," she said, making the sign of the cross. "How does Krystal even know any of these people?"

"She's seeing Tank," replied Adriana. "Who is in their club. The Gold Vipers."

Her lips tightened. "And you wonder why this happened? Didn't I tell you how dangerous these people were?"

"Ma'am, I wouldn't let anything happen to your daughter. You have my word," I tried again, hoping she'd give me a break for Adriana's sake. I could tell how much she loved her mother and I respected that. I didn't like the shit spewing out of her mouth, but I wasn't about to make a scene.

Her eyes burned into mine. "I don't care about *your* word. It's the word of the people you hang out with that I have a problem with."

I clenched my jaw. "My brothers respect women. Most of them."

"And was this guy, Breaker, one of your brothers?"

"Fuck no. He wasn't part of our crew."

"Charming vocabulary you have," she scoffed.

"I never claimed to be a saint, Mrs. Nikolas."

"Believe me, no one would never mistake you for one," she answered.

I grunted.

"Look, we don't have time to argue about this right now, Mom. We need to get down to the precinct."

"I'm coming with you," she replied, picking up her purse.

Adriana raised her hand in the air. "No, actually, I prefer that you stayed home."

Vanda's face fell. "Why?"

She let out a frustrated sigh. "Because I don't need to listen to you rail me about Trevor on the ride out there."

Vanda looked at me, her eyes full of venom. She turned back to Adriana and raised her chin. "Fine. I will drive separately."

"You don't need to come," said Adriana.

"Of course I do. Someone needs to be there for support," said Vanda.

"That someone is already going. Me," I replied.

"If you want to look out for my daughter, you'll stay out of her life," she said firmly.

"Mom!"

"I'm sorry, Adriana, but you know how I feel about bikers. I'm not going to pretend I'm happy to find the both of you together in my house."

"I thought this was my house, too," said Adriana, now looking almost as angry as me.

"Of course it is. But, you are my daughter and I am just trying to protect you."

I sighed. "I'm going upstairs to get my jacket," I said, heading for the steps.

"What is his jacket doing in your bedroom?" said Vanda shrilly.

Shaking my head, I went into her bedroom and grabbed my jacket. As I was turning around, Adriana stepped into the room.

"I'm sorry about my mother," she said, walking over to the mirror. She ran her fingers through her hair. "She can be a real pain in the ass."

I walked up behind her. "Yeah, well she's not afraid to speak her mind. I'll give that to her."

"She doesn't know you, though. So, don't let it get to you."

I grabbed her around the waist and smiled at her in the mirror. "The only thing that gets to me, Kitten, is you."

She smiled.

I kissed the side of her head. "What a nightmare, huh?" I whispered.

Adriana nodded.

Letting out a frustrated sigh, I let her go.

"I wish I would have waited for her to pull out of the parking lot," she said, looking teary-eyed again. "I feel like it's my fault."

"It's definitely not your fault, babe. Don't even go there." I reached inside my jacket for my phone. "And, don't worry, I'm sure Slammer and Tank will get her back."

She wiped a tear from under her lash. "What do you think happened?"

I couldn't tell her about The Judge. She wouldn't understand. But, I wasn't going to lie to her either. "Personally? I think it was retaliation. I think the Devil's Rangers believe we had something to do with Breaker's murder and took her."

"Did you?" she whispered.

I looked her in the eye. "I can honestly say that none of us killed him."

She let out a sigh of relief. "Okay."

"Are you two coming?" asked Vanda, standing in the doorway. She was glaring at me again.

"Yes," said Adriana, grabbing a pair of socks from her dresser.

I looked down and saw Adriana's dress still lying on the floor next to her bra. When I raised my eyes, I saw that Vanda had noticed it too, and was not happy.

I couldn't help but to dig into her. "Looks like a bomb went off in here," I said, grinning.

Vanda's eyes narrowed. "I'll wait for you outside," she said, walking away from the bedroom.

I walked over to the doorway and leaned out. "Since you're not riding with Adriana, you can certainly ride with me." I smiled evilly. I just couldn't help myself. "I don't bite."

She grunted. "Hah. I'd rather walk."

Man, she was brutal. "You sure? Riding on the back of a Harley might just put a smile on your face."

"Nothing you could do for me would *ever* put a smile on my face," she answered, heading down the stairs. "Unless it has to do with leaving my daughter alone."

I sighed.

Chapter Twenty-Nine

Adriana

When we reached the station, Trevor and I were ushered into two separate rooms. I reiterated everything that had happened the past two days, only leaving out Jason and the fact that he'd almost date-raped me. They recorded my statements with my mother sitting next to me, holding my hand. When she heard how I'd met Breaker in Griffin's, she made the sign of the cross and scolded me in front of the detectives. It was embarrassing.

"I didn't want to go inside there either," I told her. "But, Krystal insisted."

"Why did she insist?" asked Detective Stone.

"Because it was her birthday and she needed to talk to Tank."

They began asking me questions about Krystal and Tank's relationship.

"I don't know too much about it," I said. "I mean, they've been dating but she mentioned something tonight about breaking up with Tank."

Stone suddenly perked up. "She did? What was her reasoning?"

"To be honest, I think she was getting bored. Krystal doesn't like to stick with one guy too long. Plus, he's kind of bossy. At least, that's what she said. I don't see him enough to know for certain."

"You don't think she might have tried to break it off tonight and he became angry?" he asked.

"No. I mean, I guess I don't know. Um, didn't you mention that the person who called it in said she was taken by two men wearing masks?"

He nodded. "Yes, she did. But, we need to check every angle. In case Tank is somehow involved."

"To be honest, I can't imagine that he is," I replied. I could tell from the look in Tank's eyes that he really cared for her.

"You just said you didn't know him very well," reminded Stone.

"I know, but..."

"He hangs out with a rough crowd," said Stone. "They certainly aren't choir boys."

"Indeed," said my mother, sniffing. "Those bikers are all nothing but thugs."

I rolled my eyes. "Oh, for the love of God, Mom. You don't know them so give it a rest."

"I don't have to know them. And neither do you."

Arguing with her was pointless. She was so stubborn. Sighing, I turned back to Stone. "I just can't see Tank doing something like that. She said that most of the time he was like a big teddy bear toward her." I left out the part of how she was afraid to break it off with him. I just didn't believe Tank was the kind of guy who'd kidnap or hurt her.

"Yet, she wants to break up with him?" he said.

"Krystal gets bored. That's the way she is and always has been. In high school, she used to have a new boyfriend every month. So, wanting to break up with him isn't a surprise. "

He began asking me about the Gold Vipers.

"Seriously, I don't know very much about them," I said. "I just met Trevor yesterday, through Tank. All I know is that they're a club and it's like one big family."

"What's your relationship with Trevor?" asked Stone.

My mother's hand tightened on mine.

"We just met. I don't know, yet."

"Can I give you some advice?" he said, staring at me hard.

I shrugged.

"Stay away from him and the rest of his gang. We've got records on almost everyone associated with the Gold Vipers. Everything from narcotics to arson to theft. You don't want to be involved with people like that. They'll bring you down with them if you're not careful."

"What about Trevor?" asked my mother, leaning forward. "Does he have a record?"

"No, surprisingly, he doesn't. That just probably means he's good at keeping a low profile. He knows how to play that game and not get caught."

"Or, he's not playing any game and he's just a decent human being," I countered, getting angry.

Stone smirked. "He comes from trash. His father's in prison for drugs and his mother's been in and out of jail most of her life. He's in a gang of hoodlums, which is right, by the way, Ms. Nikolas," he said, nodding toward my mother. "They are really nothing but a bunch of thugs."

"See," she said, waving her finger at me. "I told you."

I sighed. "Just because they are doesn't mean Trevor is."

"Defend him all you want, but ask yourself this – why would he want to be associated with people who continually break the law if he's such a decent guy?" asked Stone.

"I don't know, maybe because he has nobody else?" I mumbled, rubbing my forehead. "You know, I thought we were here to talk about finding Krystal and Breaker?"

"We are," he said, shuffling papers. "Which reminds me –"

Another officer walked through the doorway and motioned for Stone. "We have some information."

"Oh. Good." He smiled at us and stood up. "I'll be right back."

"You heard what that man said about this gang," said Vanda, after he left. "They are nothing but trouble."

"I know what he said, but Trevor is a good guy."

"How do you know?" she said angrily. "You keep defending someone you don't know, Adriana."

"Because sometimes, you just do," I replied angrily.

"You've only known him for two days."

"Yeah, so? It's not like we're getting married."

"You may as well after what went on in your bedroom," she mumbled, looking at me out of the corner of her eye.

I sighed. "So what? I'm twenty-one years old. I'm not a child."

"I know, but –"

"Mom, you have to learn to trust me," I said, grabbing her hand. "I know Trevor is part of this gang, but he's much more than that. I can feel it. I can also feel that he would never do anything to hurt me."

"You've just met. How do you really know?" she asked, looking weary.

"I don't know. It's something in my gut, I guess."

She sighed. "You're all I have, Adriana. If anything happened to you, I… I don't know what I'd do."

I squeezed her hand. "I know, Mom. But, you don't have to worry about me."

"I will *always* worry about you," she replied, blinking back tears.

"I know, but learn to trust me. Okay?"

She let out ragged sigh. "I do trust you. It's him I don't trust."

"Try? For me?"

"I will try, but if he hurts you, so help me…"

The door opened up and Stone walked in. The look on his face was grave.

"What's going on?" I asked.

He sat down across from me. "I have some troubling news."

My heart stopped. "What is it?"

Stone put his hand over mine. "We found your friend, Krystal. She's been murdered."

"What?!" I shrieked, pulling my hand away. I covered my mouth. "She's been murdered?" I began to cry. "No! This has to be a mistake!"

"Krystal's mother has already confirmed that it's her," he said. "I'm so sorry."

"Where did they find her?" asked my mother, who had her arm around me as I sobbed.

"She was found in the parking lot of Griffin's. She was… rolled up in a blanket."

"Oh, my God," I cried, picturing it. "Those bastards!"

"It gets worse. From what it sounds like, whoever left her there was sending a message. In fact," he sighed, "I probably shouldn't even tell you this, but I want you to know what kind of people we are dealing with."

"Tell me what?" I said hoarsely, waiting for him to continue.

"Someone carved the words 'Revenge Is Sweet' on her stomach," he said, his eyes hardening.

"What does that mean?" asked my mother.

"I believe this was payback for Breaker's murder. Look," he said, pinning me with his eyes. "This could have just as easily been you. Hell, maybe it was supposed to be, since Breaker was obviously obsessed with you."

"What?" cried my mother. "You think they were trying to target Adriana and got Krystal, instead?"

"It's possible. There's obviously a war going on between these two gangs and an innocent girl was murdered."

"That's it!" cried Vanda. "You are never seeing that man again. Krystal is dead and I'm not losing you, Adriana. Promise me you won't see Trevor again. Promise me!"

Stone handed me a box of tissues. "I'd have to agree with your mother. Especially now that there's a murder investigation going on. You need to stay as far away from this character as you can."

The pain in my heart seemed unbearable as I pictured Krystal's beautiful, smiling face. We'd been best friends for so many years. Now she was gone, and for what? Revenge? *Because of me?*

"Fine… I promise," I mumbled, wiping my tears. "I won't go near any of them."

"You're making a wise choice," said Stone. "You know that, don't you?"

The only thing I did know was that my best friend was dead… and nothing else mattered.

Chapter Thirty

Adriana

Krystal's funeral was two weeks later, after the autopsy. It was revealed that she'd been raped and then strangled. Unfortunately, they didn't have enough evidence to arrest anyone, so the investigation was still open.

Trevor and Tank both attended the funeral, even though Krystal's mother had tried banning anyone associated with the Gold Vipers. She blamed them directly for her daughter's murder. When the time came, however, she allowed them to attend, too grief-stricken to care about anything else other than the fact that she was burying her daughter.

When it was time for me to speak during the eulogy, my eyes met Trevor's for a brief second. He nodded, but I looked away, my heart heavy for everything I'd lost in the last two weeks.

"I met Krystal in the sixth grade," I said, reading from the piece of paper in front of me. I knew the words by heart, but I couldn't look at anyone. I knew I'd start to cry. "I was new in school and very nervous. After the teacher introduced me in class, I went to go take a seat when a boy stuck out his foot. I tripped, landing on my face, dropping my books and everything else. Of course, everyone laughed. Well, everyone but the teacher and Krystal, I guess." I smiled through my tears and went on. "She beat him up after school that day. Actually punched out one of his teeth, because of the way he'd tried to humiliate me. The funny thing was, they were going steady."

Some people chuckled.

"That was Krystal, though. She had a heart and she'd stick up for you, no matter what." I sniffled. "If you were her friend, you'd be one for life. If you were a guy in her life, well, you didn't want to piss her off or you might have ended up with dentures."

More chuckles.

"Anyway," I looked up. "Although she's gone, I know she's looking down at us today, wondering if her hair was done right or they used the right color of lipstick." I smiled sadly and looked over at Tiffany and Claudia. "Remember when she went through that phase of wearing blue lipstick? I still don't know what that was about."

They both nodded, smiling through their tears.

I took a deep breath. "Anyway, Krystal, we're going to miss seeing you laugh and smile, but we'll always feel you in our hearts. Always. I love you and I already miss you so very much," I said, my voice cracking. "I only wish I would have told you how much when you were still alive."

My eyes were blurred with tears and I couldn't read the rest. Wiping my face with the back of my hand, I picked up my sheet of paper and hurried away from the podium.

"You did good, honey," whispered my mom as I sat down next to her. "I'm sure Krystal thought so, too."

I didn't say anything, I was too choked up.

When the funeral was over, we all drove to the cemetery, where she was laid to rest. As I put a rose on her coffin, I looked up to find Trevor standing on the other side, watching me. I had to admit, he looked incredibly handsome, especially in the dark suit he was wearing.

I quickly looked away.

"I have to get back to the shop," said Vanda, as we walked back to the car with Jim, who'd also attended the funeral. They'd already been on a couple more dates, and were becoming very close. I could tell by the way that she looked at him.

"I'll drive you," he said. "That way, Adriana can go to the reception."

"Thanks," she said, digging into her purse. "Here are the keys. Are you okay to drive?"

"Yes. Of course."

She looked past me and her eyes hardened. "I still can't believe those two had the audacity to show up."

I turned around to see Trevor and Tank walking toward their motorcycles. Tank's expression was unreadable now, but I had seen tears in his eyes when they lowered her casket. He'd definitely had feelings for her.

"I can't believe they're riding bikes in this weather," said Jim. "It must be forty degrees. That's got to be cold."

I shrugged.

"He didn't try talking to you, did he?" she asked as we reached the two cars, which were parked next to each other.

"No," I said. He'd been respectful to my wishes, even though he hadn't understood them.

"So, that's it? You don't want to see me again?" he'd said, after I'd given him the news.

"I just can't see you again."

"Why?"

"Because of what happened. Krystal is dead. DEAD. I can't get caught up in that kind of... world."

"You know I'd never put you in any kind of danger."

"Trevor, your entire world is 'danger'. Whether you want to admit it or not."

"I'm not ready to let you go," he'd said, his eyes burning into mine. "You've gotten under my skin. You're all I think about."

"You know what I'm thinking about? My best friend. She's dead – and why? Because of some senseless gang warfare she didn't want any part of, either. I don't want to be next. I don't want to die."

"You aren't going to die."

"How can you be certain?"

"I won't let them near you."

"That's a gallant thought, but you can't protect me every hour of the day."

"They're going to pay for what they did and then, I promise, you won't have to worry about it."

"See, that's exactly what I do have to worry about. Retaliation. First them and then you. It's going to go on and on. I just want to live my life without having to worry about getting kidnapped or shot, Trevor. Don't you understand?"

He sighed.

"Trevor, please... respect my wishes and... stay away from me."

"That's just it. I don't know if I can do that."

"You have to try. If you're not even willing, then you're not the man I thought you were."

"Ouch."

"I'm serious."

He'd finally relented, even though it had been hard for both of us. I knew I wasn't in love with him, but there was something between us. Something fierce.

She nodded. "Good. I'm glad."

I sighed. "I'll see you tonight."

"Be careful. Don't drink and drive."

"Yes, mother," I said, my voice hollow.

"Don't drink too much and drive," corrected Jim, smiling. "One glass of wine won't hurt."

I winked at him and got into the car.

Mom waved at me as she slid into Jim's car.

Stealing another glance across the parking lot at Trevor, I tried ignoring the pangs in my chest. I wasn't a fool. I knew that I longed to be with him, even after everything that had happened. Feel his arms around me. But, it was over and both of us had to accept it.

    I started the engine and drove to the reception.

Chapter Thirty-One

Adriana

The reception was held at a local bar. As I walked toward the entrance, I ran into Detective Stone. I'd seen both him and Detective Williams at the funeral, but was surprised to see him at the reception.

"Hello, Adriana," he said, holding the door for me.

"Detective Stone. I didn't know you were going to be here."

"Please, call me Jeremy."

I smiled. "Sure."

"I wanted to pay my respects," he said, walking behind me. "How have you been holding up?"

I glanced at him over my shoulder. "It's been hard."

"I can only imagine."

"How is the case going?" I asked as he moved next to me.

"Slow."

"Can't you find any DNA or fiber matches to convict any of the Devil's Rangers?"

He grinned. "You've been watching CSI?"

"Of course," I said, smiling sheepishly.

"Well, they're still working on it. That's all I can really say," he said as we entered the area that was reserved for the reception. I noticed Tiffany, Monica, and Amber were already there, ordering drinks.

"Thanks for coming," said Krystal's mother, Bonnie, who looked like she was about ready to start crying all over again. "Both of you."

"Of course," I said, hugging her.

"You, too, Detective. Have you found the people who've done this yet?"

"Please, just call me Jeremy. We're still working on it. You'll be the first to know if we do, though."

"I'm counting on it," she said, blowing her nose.

"Hi, Adriana," said Tiffany, walking over with two glasses. "Here, I bought you a rum and Coke. Figured you'd need it after giving that speech. You did great, by the way. I was bawling my eyes out."

"Thanks, Tiff. I missed the last part of it," I said, taking the drink from her. "I was too choked up to continue."

"How could you not be? At least you had the balls to get up there. I'm sure Krystal was proud of you, though."

"I hope so," I said, getting choked up again myself.

"And, who is this?" she asked, smiling up at Jeremy.

I was going to introduce him as Detective Stone, when he jumped in.

"Who me? I'm Jeremy Stone," he said, smiling.

"Are you two...?" she asked, pointing to both of us.

"No," I said quickly, realizing what she meant. "We're not dating."

He laughed.

She smiled at Jeremy. "I wasn't sure. You're not wearing a ring and I've never seen you before. I know that."

Oh, my God, she's interested in him, I thought, not sure if I should be amused or horrified.

"Nope. No ring," he said, holding up his left hand. "Not anymore, at least."

"Oh, were you married before?" she asked.

"Engaged. I guess you could say it fell through."

"Well, you know what they say – if it's not meant to be, it's not meant to be," said Tiffany, taking a drink of her Screwdriver. "You'll probably find someone much better."

It was then that I realized he was actually a very nice looking man. I hadn't thought much about it before, but I could see why Tiffany was interested. He was tall, with brown hair, caramel colored eyes, and a goatee. I pegged him to be in his late twenties and he obviously kept in very good shape.

"How did you know Krystal?" she asked.

As he began explaining, I glanced over to the bar and noticed that Trevor was standing next to it, ordering a beer. My stomach knotted up.

What was he doing here?

"Excuse me," I said, moving around my friends and toward him. When I reached the bar, Trevor turned to me, smiling.

"What are you doing here?" I said in a not-so-friendly voice.

"Well, hello to you, too," he said, the smile falling.

I looked around. "Is Tank here, too?"

"No. He's taking it pretty hard. He just wanted to be alone."

I stared at him for a few seconds, my foot tapping anxiously. I had to admit that he looked so handsome that I wanted to jump his bones again. But, I was more pissed than horny. "You shouldn't be here, you know."

He frowned. "Why? I knew her too, you know. I'm just here to pay my respects."

"You did that at the cemetery."

He grunted and shook his head.

"What?' I asked.

"Why are you being such a bitch?" he said angrily.

"Excuse me?" I said, shocked.

"You heard me."

My eyes narrowed. "Maybe because you bring that out in me."

"Why? I haven't done anything to you," he said, taking a drink of his beer.

"You're here, Trevor."

"Yeah? Why is that a problem?"

I lowered my voice. "I thought you were going to stay away?"

He laughed coldly. "Oh, I see. You think this is about you. Well, Kitten, it's not. This is about paying my respects to Krystal, who I was friends with too, believe it or not."

"Really?" I snapped. "You're not here for *anything* else?"

"No, I'm not. And," he sneered, "in case you don't remember, *you* approached me, I didn't approach you."

I clenched my jaw. I was so angry. I wanted to slap the asshole grin right off of his face.

"So, feel free to unapproach me," he said, looking away.

Trying not to make a scene, I turned around and walked back over to the others.

"Isn't that Trevor Larson?" asked Jeremy.

"Yes," I said, taking a drink of my cocktail. "Yes, it is."

"Is everything okay?" he asked, leaning closer me.

I looked over at Trevor, who now was staring at Jeremy, looking pissed.

"It's fine," I said, looking away.

"Adriana, we're going across the street to Gibby's later. You want to join us?" asked Tiffany.

"I don't think so," I said, staring down at my drink.

"Come on," she said. "Just for a couple of drinks and some dancing. You know that's what Krystal would have wanted. To see us together and having fun. This will be our big send-off, for her."

"I don't know…"

"Come on, I'll even drive you home," she said. "If that's what you're worried about."

"Right, you drive? You'd better quit drinking now," I said, smirking.

"Tell you what," said Jeremy. "I'll drive all four of you home, if you want. I don't work tomorrow and I have nothing better to do."

"You would?" squealed Tiffany. She grabbed his arm. "Thank you *so* much."

I sighed. "You don't have to do this."

"I know. But, I want to," he said. "Like Tiffany said, this will be your tribute to Krystal. You may as well have fun."

I saw the way he kept glancing at Tiffany and wondered if he was doing it for other reasons as well.

"Well, I'm game then," I said, still watching Trevor from the corner of my eye. He was talking to Krystal's mother, now, and she was smiling at him.

"I'm going to grab a soda, does anyone need anything?" asked Jeremy.

"No, I think we're all good," said Monica, holding up her drink.

"So, who is this Trevor Larson?" whispered Tiffany as Jeremy walked away. "He's hot."

"Somebody you want to stay away from," I said, taking another drink.

"Are you sure?" she said, licking her lips. "I wouldn't mind inviting him over to Gibby's with us. Something tells me he knows how to move those hips like a boss."

An image of Trevor moving his hips between mine flashed through my brain and I felt a quiver down below. Forcing those intimate thoughts away, I cleared my throat. "That's Raptor," I said. "He's part of the Gold Vipers."

"Raptor, the biker?" she said. "Oh, yeah. Didn't you and he…?"

"Almost," I said, turning to her. "Why are you asking about him when you have your eye on Jeremy?"

She grinned. "He's cute, too. But, he's too serious. The only kind of serious I want tonight, is a seriously good fuck."

"Is that all you ever think about?" asked Monica, shaking her head. "I mean, we're at a funeral."

"This isn't the funeral. It's the celebration of our friend's life. We're supposed to remember her with fondness and have fun. That's what she would have wanted," said Tiffany.

"She's right," said Amber, who was texting on her phone. "Although, I can't believe you're already thinking about who you're going to have sex with tonight. It's not even seven o'clock."

"I like planning ahead," she said, taking a drink of her cocktail.

"Look at you, Amber. You're probably setting up a booty call yourself right now," said Monica.

"This is different. It's Paul. My fiancé," she replied. "Sex is a given."

"Why isn't he here?" I asked.

She shrugged. "He's working. Like usual."

"Are you still going to Gibby's?" I asked.

She nodded and put her phone away. "Yeah, for a little while. I'm not going to drink much, though."

"What about you?" I asked Monica.

"My mom is babysitting. I'm definitely going out and partying my ass off tonight. Especially, if he's driving."

Jeremy returned with a soda.

"So, what's it like being a detective?" asked Tiffany, sidling up to him again.

He began talking about his job and I listened with one ear, while keeping my eye on Trevor, who seemed to be in the middle of a conversation with Tiffany's aunt, Jenna, who was a beauty consultant for a popular makeup company. Jenna, who Tiffany had always referred to as a 'cougar', was definitely intrigued with whatever they were discussing.

"That's fascinating," said Tiffany, who was also hanging on to every word Jeremy was saying. "What made you want to get into law enforcement?"

I didn't hear his response because Jenna was laughing at something Trevor had said. It started a fire in my stomach. An angry, jealous one.

I finished my rum and Coke. "Anyone else need another drink?" I asked.

"Sure," said Tiffany, holding up her glass, which was almost empty. "You know what I like."

"Yeah, me too," said Monica. "I'll take a Vodka Collins."

I walked to the bar and ordered the drinks. As I waited, Jenna walked away from Trevor and up to the bar. I had to admit, with her long blonde hair, flawless skin, and lithe figure, she didn't look anywhere near thirty-eight. She looked like a twenty-something Pamela Anderson double.

"Hi, Adriana," she said, smiling at me somberly. "How are you holding up, kiddo?"

I shrugged. "I'm okay. What about you?"

"It's been tough. Really tough. Bonnie is barely holding on. She blames herself for not being a better mother to Krystal."

"That's not what killed her," I said, although I knew Bonnie hadn't been the best parent. Krystal had gotten away with murder.

"No, but if she would have been a stricter parent when she was growing up, things might have been different." She shook her head. "Bonnie let that girl get away with too much."

"Yeah, but that doesn't mean she wouldn't have been where she was that night."

"Maybe. Maybe not. Guess, we'll never know."

"I guess."

She sighed and looked over at Trevor.

"You know that guy?" I asked, nodding toward him.

She smiled. "No, but I'd love to, you know what I mean?"

I certainly did.

"He's a biker," I said.

"I know. We were talking about it. I told him that I just bought a Harley Switchback and he was impressed."

"I bet. I didn't know you were into bikes," I said trying to stifle the green monster growing inside of me. Deep down, I knew there was no reason for me to be jealous. I had no claim on Trevor and she was a very nice woman. If they got together, that was none of my business.

"My ex-boyfriend got me interested."

"What happened to him?"

She sighed. "Found out he was married."

"You didn't know?"

"Well," she smiled. "I did. He said they were getting divorced, so I thought they were separated. Come to find out, they really weren't either."

The bartender set my drinks down. "Here's a tray. I doubt you can carry all four drinks by yourself."

"You're right. Thanks," I said, handing her the money.

"It's an open bar," said the woman. "For another hour, at least."

"Oh, well, here's a tip," I said, handing her a couple of dollars.

"Thanks, hon." She turned to Jenna. "What can I get for you?"

"I'll take two Michelobs. One for me and one for that tall drink of water, over there," she said, turning to smile at Trevor, who I noticed was watching us.

Feeling angry again, I looked away.

Jenna turned back to me and sighed. "You must think I'm a horrible aunt."

"What do you mean?" I asked.

She smiled grimly. "Because my mind is in the gutter at my niece's funeral."

"People cope with things differently," I said, a little guilty of it myself.

She put her arm around me. "I agree. In fact, I've always coped with grief by turning to intimacy. The touch of another can sometimes ease the pain of loss. It's also a good reminder that we're still alive and that every second matters, because you never know when your time is up."

"I guess... that makes sense to me."

"To me it does. That's why I don't feel guilty about setting my sights on Raptor tonight." She winked. "Something tells me he just might be my salvation."

"And you know that after just talking to him for a few minutes?"

She grinned wickedly. "To be honest, I don't care what comes out of his mouth. It's what goes into his mouth later that interests me. Thanks, doll," she said to the bartender, who set two beers down in front of us. She handed her a five. "That's for you."

"Thanks," said the bartender, shoving it into her front pocket. She leaned forward. "And good luck with that young man. I wouldn't mind going home with him myself tonight."

Jenna laughed. "You'd better get in line," she answered before walking back toward Trevor.

Sighing, I picked up the tray of drinks and went the other way.

Chapter Thirty-Two

R*A*PTOR

I watched Adriana and Jenna talking at the bar, and had to hide my grin. Adriana looked like she was ready to spit bullets whenever she looked at me.

"Oh, she's pissed," whispered Jenna, close to my ear when she returned with our beers.

Jenna and I went way back. She'd dated Slammer five years ago and we'd always gotten along. When she'd learned what had happened to her niece, she'd rushed down to Griffin's and I'd told her everything, including what had happened between me and Adriana.

"Why?" I asked. "Because I'm still here?"

"Because, I'm making her jealous."

"You are?"

"Yes," she said, snuggling up to me.

"I don't think that's a good idea."

"Are you kidding? She's going to realize how much she wants you and believe me, you're going to be thanking me later."

My eyebrow arched. "Really? Because when men get jealous, it doesn't usually work that way. They get pissed and leave."

"No, you don't," she said. "In fact, I'm pretty sure if you saw a guy hitting on Adriana, you'd want to beat the shit out of him."

"Look, there's nothing between us. Not anymore," I said, not believing my own words. The truth was, I wanted her more than ever. When I'd seen her at the funeral, wearing another black dress and the same sapphire necklace, it had reminded me of that night in her bedroom. Then I'd pictured her straddling my face while I was looking up at her gorgeous body, and I knew I was going straight to Hell. Especially knowing that I had to have been the only asshole in church sporting wood.

"I don't believe that for one second and either do you."

I shrugged. "Believe what you want."

Jenna frowned. "Why is the cop here? They walked in together. Did you see that?"

"Yeah, but they didn't arrive here together."

"It looks like Tiffany has her eye on him, anyway. He's cute." She waved at Tiffany, who waved back.

I took another swig of beer.

"So, what are you going to do?"

"Finish this and leave."

She tilted her head. "Don't you want to try and win her back?"

"I never had her to begin with. If I did, she wouldn't have given up so easily."

Jenna sighed. "I've met Vanda. She's not an easy woman to stand up to."

"Adriana is twenty-one. She's an adult."

"She may look like an adult, but nobody has given her the chance to act like one."

I smirked. "I tried. Believe me, I did."

"I'm sure you did. But, I think you need to try again."

"What do you propose I do? Show up at her house? Serenade her? I do that and I'll just get my ass chewed out."

"No. That's a waste of time. You need to act tonight. While she's got that fire burning in her belly."

"How do you know she's got a fire burning in her belly?"

"By the way she keeps stealing glances over here. The girl still has it bad for you, Raptor. She doesn't know whether to slap or kiss you."

"Hmm… Well, what do you suggest I do?"

This time Jenna was the one smiling wickedly. "Nothing. Let me take care of it."

Chapter Thirty-Three

Adriana

An hour later, Tiffany announced that it was time to go across the street to Gibby's.

"Okay," I said. "It's getting really crowded in here anyway."

"It's going to be more crowded at Gibby's," warned Jeremy, who'd opened his tie and now seemed very relaxed.

"But at least we can dance," I said, feeling absolutely no pain. I'd just finished my third drink and even Trevor's presence wasn't bothering me anymore. Well, not as much. After the second drink, I kept telling myself that if those two hooked up, then good riddance. After my third drink, I'd decided that I needed to rethink my own rule of hooking up. Possibly find a guy who might make me forget all about Trevor. Someone tall, dark, and very well-endowed.

"I want to dance, too. Let's go and say goodbye to Bonnie and go over there," said Monica, grabbing me and Amber by the arms. Just like me, she was also feeling quite good.

"Thanks for coming," said Bonnie, hugging each of us when we found her.

"Of course and, we're so sorry for your loss," said Tiffany, smiling sadly. "And ours. We're losing a great friend. One of the best. We're sure going to miss that girl."

Bonnie's lips trembled. "Me, too," she squeaked. "Me, too."

"I'm sorry my mother couldn't make it," I said when she hugged me. "She's going to call you tomorrow."

"She made it to the funeral. That's enough. Plus, she's been there for me these last couple of weeks. Bringing me food, calling everyone. I don't know how I can thank her enough."

"You don't have to," I told Bonnie. "She wanted to help."

She nodded. "Well, I appreciate it."

"I'm sorry for your loss, Ms. Blake," said Jeremy, shaking her hand.

"Just find them," she said. "Please. Find the people who did this and put them away."

"Believe me, I'll do my best."

"Are you leaving?" asked Jenna, coming up behind me?"

"We're going across the street," said Monica. "To Gibby's. You want to join us?"

"Let me ask my new friend," she said, her blue eyes sparkling. "Something tells me he'll want to go dancing, too."

"You mean Trevor?" I said, looking around. "Did he leave?"

"No, he's using the bathroom," she said, smiling. "I didn't realize you knew his real name."

"Lucky guess," I said, forcing a smile. He'd obviously told her his real name, too. I looked at Tiffany. "Let's go. I'm getting really warm in here."

"Okay," she said, waving to Jenna and Bonnie. "Have a good night."

"You too," said Bonnie. "Drive safely."

"Jeremy is driving all of us home," Tiffany said, sliding her arm through his. "Aren't you?"

Jeremy smiled. "Yep. That I am. I don't know what I'm getting myself into, but it's too late to back out now, right?"

"You're damn right," said Tiffany, snuggling up to him. "You're going to have fun, though. We'll make sure of it. Right, ladies?"

"You bet," said Monica. "Ready, Adriana?"

I saw Trevor walk out of the bathroom and head toward us, or rather, Jenna. I quickly turned around and started for the exit. "I'm more than ready. In fact, I'll meet you over there."

Chapter Thirty-Four

Adriana

Gibby's was jam-packed when we walked in. Apparently, it was Ladies Night, and all shots were half-off.

"Let's dance and *then* drink," said Tiffany, pulling me and Jeremy toward the large dance floor, while Monica and Amber used the bathroom. He'd left his jacket and tie in the car and now looked more like a regular guy just out to have fun. "Do you like Hip Hop music, Jeremy?" she cried, over the loud music.

"Not really," he hollered back. "But, I'm willing to try."

"What kind of music do you like?" I asked.

"Rock-n-Roll. Jazz. Country. Anything but... Hip Hop."

"That's too bad," said Tiffany, rolling her hips with the music. "Because I *love* Hip Hop. It makes me so... frisky."

His eyes widened and then he laughed. "Maybe I haven't given Hip Hop enough of a chance."

She moved closer to him, until they were chin-to-forehead. "Relax and move your hips," she said, putting her hands on his waist. "I'll help you learn how to like it."

"I'm sure you will," he said, putting his hands around her hips.

She gave him a sexy laugh.

I suddenly felt like a third wheel. I backed away from the dance floor and then took off toward the bar. When I saw Trevor and Jenna waiting in line for a drink, I stopped dead in my tracks.

Dammit.

They were so beautiful together. Both blond and dazzling under the strobe lights.

Trevor had taken his hair out of the ponytail, and his jacket and tie were gone. He reminded me of a sexy rock star standing there with his supermodel girlfriend on his arm. I suddenly felt very dowdy in my black dress. Jenna was also wearing a black dress, but hers emphasized her breasts while mine were drowning in fabric.

"Oh, hey," she said, noticing me. She slipped her arms through Trevor's and grinned. "Hope you don't mind that we followed you over here?"

"That's okay," I said, minding very much. I forced a smile. "It's a great place to… unwind."

"Definitely," said Jenna. She reached up and unbuttoned two of Trevor's buttons, exposing his tan chest. "In fact, I think it's time for this hunk of yumminess to unwind." She slipped her fingers under his dark blue shirt and looked at me. "I don't know what it is but I just can't seem to keep my hands off of him."

"Nobody seems to be stopping you, either," I said, gritting my teeth.

Just then the music slowed to a sexy beat and Jenna sucked in her breath. "I love this song. Forget the drinks. Come on, dance with me."

Trevor's eyes met mine.

I scowled and looked away.

"Come on," she said, pulling his arm. "Let's go and have some fun."

I didn't hear his reply, but I watched her drag his ass to the dance floor without any resistance. Then she slipped her arms around his neck and pulled him so close that I couldn't stand to watch them anymore.

Seething, I made my way over to the bar and bought myself a shot of peach schnapps.

To you, Krystal, I thought, slamming it down.

"Would you like another one?" asked the bartender, a heavyset guy wearing a Stetson.

"Yes. One more," I said, sliding the shot gas back to him.

"What is that?" asked the guy standing next to me.

I looked at him. He had soft brown eyes and a boyish smile. "It's just peach schnapps."

He grimaced. "Oh, not that."

I smiled. "What's wrong with it? Too girly?"

He chuckled. "No, I used to love the taste, before I spent an entire weekend puking my guts out after drinking a bottle. Watch out for that stuff, it'll kick you in the ass later."

"Thanks for the advice," I said, as the bartender slid another shot toward me. "I doubt I'll drink an entire bottle, but I'll keep it in mind."

"Now, tequila... that's what you should be drinking. Are you driving tonight, or is your boyfriend?" he asked.

"I'm not driving and I don't have a boyfriend."

He smiled and straightened up. "Well, in that case, how about we both have a shot together? My treat?"

I slammed the second shot of peach schnapps and set it on the bar. "How about... we dance?" I said, licking my lips. "Then you can buy me a shot."

His smile grew wider. He set his beer down on the bar. "Watch this for me, will you, Hank?"

"Sure thing," said the bartender.

"And put her other two shots on my tab."

I grinned. "Well, thank you... what was your name?"

"It's Dan."

I held out my hand. "I'm Adriana."

"Pretty name," he said, shaking it. "And well deserving."

I giggled, the peach schnapps warming my tummy and everything else.

"Just to warn you, I'm not the best dancer," he said, following me out to the dance floor.

"It's okay," I said, turning to him. "I won't judge if you won't."

He slid his arms around my waist. "If I said I've already judged you to be the prettiest girl in this bar, would you laugh in my face?"

I was about to do just that when I noticed Trevor staring at me from across the dance floor. He was scowling.

"Not at all," I said, noting that Jenna was standing in front of him, grinding her ass against his crotch. Obviously, he wasn't angry about that and he certainly wasn't stopping her from doing it, either. Clenching my jaw, I slid my arms up to Dan's neck and forced myself to smile. "You have gorgeous eyes. Has anyone ever told you that?"

He grinned. "Thank you."

I stole another glance over Dan's shoulder at Trevor, and almost choked. He was storming toward us, like an angry bull.

Dan noticed him as well. "Can I help you?" he asked, letting me go.

"I'm cutting in," said Trevor. He grabbed my arm.

"Stop it," I hissed. "Go back to Jenna."

"I don't *want* her," he said, his eyes burning into mine.

"Right. I think you only want what you can't have."

He looked like I'd slapped him. "Fuck you."

"No, fuck you!" I snapped, pulling my arm away.

"You're drunk," he said, his voice harsh and angry.

I raised my chin. "I'm not drunk. I'm… having fun. I'm also reconsidering my rule about one-night stands."

Dan's face lit up.

Trevor grabbed my arm again, his fingers gripping me hard. "I'm taking you home before you do something stupid."

"Excuse me… do you two know each other?" asked Dan.

"What gave you that idea?" said Trevor with a sneer. "Back off, genius. She's mine."

"I'm *not* yours," I said, pulling away again.

"Would you stop playing games, Adriana?"

"I'm not the one playing them."

"What's going on over here?" said Jeremy, suddenly at my side.

"Nothing," I said, backing away. "Nothing is going on."

"Larson, what the hell kind of shit are you starting now?" snarled Jeremy, getting into his face.

"Fuck you, Stone."

"You need to leave," ordered Jeremy, as I turned and headed toward the exit.

"Adriana!" hollered Trevor, over the music.

Chapter Thirty-Five

RAPTOR

As Adriana ran out of the bar, I attempted to follow her when that fuck-nut, Stone, got in my way.

"Leave her be," he said.

"Why don't you mind your own fucking business?" I said, glaring at him.

He clenched his jaw. "She doesn't want to see you anymore."

"Then she can tell me that. Not you."

"Enough," said Jenna, getting between us. She turned to me. "Go find her. From the look in her eyes, she wants really you to."

It certainly didn't look that way to me. But I knew women were complicated and I trusted Jenna's judgment.

I turned around and raced out of the bar, ready to pummel Stone if he tried stopping me. When I reached the parking lot, it was dark, but I could see Adriana running across the street to the other parking lot. Swearing, I ran after her.

"Adriana!' I hollered, as she unlocked the door to her car.

"Leave me alone!" she yelled, getting into it. She slammed the door shut.

I reached the car and began hollering at her. "You shouldn't be driving! You've had too much to drink!"

She flipped me off.

"Stone's going to arrest you!" I shouted at the window. "You'll get a DWI!"

That brought her to her senses. She scowled and turned off the engine.

"Come on. I'll drive you home," I said loudly.

She opened the car door and got out. "No, you won't," she said, locking it. "I'll get a ride from Stone."

"Fuck that," I said. "He's not giving you a ride home. I am."

"The hell you are," she said, shivering.

"Where's your jacket?"

She nodded to her car.

"Give me your keys," I demanded, holding out my hand. "I'll give you a ride home."

"No."

Before she could respond, I grabbed them from her. "Get in the car, or I swear to God, I'll pick you up and throw you inside myself. You know I'll do it."

She groaned angrily. "Fine. You want to drive me home? Then drive me home. I don't fucking care," she said, storming over to the passenger side of the car.

I watched her get in and then I got in.

"Put your seatbelt on."

She snapped it on angrily.

I started the engine and we began to drive.

"So, you're not going to say anything?" I said after a few minutes of silence.

"I've got nothing to say to you," she said, putting her coat on.

"Why are you so pissed off?"

She didn't reply.

Sighing, I turned on the radio. "Any requests?" I grunted. "A ballad, perhaps. You seem to like dancing to those. Especially with dipshit hipsters."

She laughed coldly. "You should talk. Oh, that's right. You two weren't dancing. You were having dry sex."

I snorted. "Dry sex?"

"Yes. Dry sex."

"What in the hell is that?"

"Dirty fucking dancing."

"Did you see me dancing?"

"No, but I saw Jenna shoving her ass against you, and you seemed to be enjoying it."

"How do you know I was enjoying it?"

She rolled her eyes. "You certainly weren't stopping her."

"I wasn't even paying attention to Jenna. I had my mind on other things," I said, taking a detour.

Chapter Thirty-Six

Adriana

I'd closed my eyes for a few minutes but opened them when I noticed that we were driving down a bumpy, gravel road, surrounded by trees.

"Where are we going?" I asked, sitting up straight.

He ignored me.

"Trevor?"

The road ended near a lake and he turned into an empty parking lot. There was a sign that read: "Prairie Lake Boat Launch, Private Property."

"What are we doing here?" I asked, not happy.

He parked the car, rolled down the windows, and then flipped through the radio channels until he located a song he seemed to like. It was an older tune by Nickelback, "Savin' Me."

"What in the hell are you doing?" I said, watching him get out.

He came around and opened up my door.

"Let's go," he said, holding out his hand.

I glared up at him. "No. This isn't funny. I want you to take me home. Now."

He grabbed my arm and pulled me out of the car.

"What the hell, Trevor?" I said, as he put his arms tightly around me and started dancing.

"I need you to explain something."

"What?" I said, feeling my stomach heat up as his hands slid slowly over hips. I knew I shouldn't be letting him do it, but I couldn't help myself. As angry as I was, I knew that I still wanted him.

"Explain what this 'dry sex' is," he whispered against my neck, the warmth of his breath on my skin, almost killing me.

I swallowed. I wasn't sure that it was even a real term, it had just popped into my head. "You know what it is."

He pulled my hips against his. I could feel his hardness pressing against my stomach. "You know what I prefer? Wet, hot sex," he whispered, dragging his lips across my neck, stopping at my ear. "My cock prefers it too," he said, nipping my ear lobe.

I closed my eyes.

He slid one of his hands up to my breast and began tracing a ring around my nipple with his thumb. I cursed myself for wearing such a thin bra. "What about you, Kitten? Don't you like it deep… and wet?"

"Yes," I said breathlessly.

He pinched the nub through the fabric. "You cold, darlin'? Because your nipple could cut glass right now."

I moaned as he pinched it harder and then moved to the other one.

"Mm... What do you know, this one's cold, too," Trevor said in a husky voice. He unbuttoned the front of my dress and slid his hand into my silk bra. "Let me help you warm up," he said, bending his face down. He pushed the material aside and took my nipple into his mouth. He swirled his tongue around the nub and then sucked, sending a shiver of pleasure all the way down to my clit.

Moaning, I moved my hand to his pants and touched his penis, desperate to feel it inside of me. I was so turned on that I didn't care about the consequences. I needed this man to fuck me.

"Uh, uh, uh," he said, stepping back. He turned me around, pushed my hair to the side, and began kissing my neck.

I closed my eyes again, enjoying his lips on my skin. He slid his hands to my breasts and pulled me closer. I could feel his hard-on pressed up against my butt.

"Is this dry sex?" he growled against my neck as he ground his hips into my ass, taunting me with his hard cock. "Or, is it more like this..." He bent me over the hood of the car and grabbed my hips, pushing my dress up. Then he began humping me through his pants, sending a swirl of tingling, tightening desire to my pelvis.

"Trevor," I panted, feeling his erection hit my opening, driving my insane. "I can't take this anymore. Take out your cock and fuck me with it."

He stopped moving and slid his fingers into my panties. He shoved one inside of my hole and I moaned as he pulled it out and did it again. "You really want me to fuck you, Kitten?" he said. "You sure that's what you really want?"

"Yes," I gasped as he slid a second one in. "Please."

He added a second finger. "I don't know. Are you wet enough?"

I was as wet as a fucking Tsunami. "You know I am," I said, spreading my hips wider, so he had better access.

"Mm… I think we can make you wetter," he murmured into my ear. He slid a finger up to my clit and began to rub it.

"Yes," I gasped, grinding my mound against his hand. Panting, I reached behind and rubbed my hand against his hard-on. "Take it out. I need to feel it."

I heard him unzip his pants and fumble with his boxers. Then he took my hand and guided me to his cock.

"I need this," I whispered, wrapping my hand around it. If felt so thick. So powerful. The thought of it between my legs, thrusting inside of me, was enough to blow a fuse in my head. "Can I suck it?" I whispered, sliding my hand back and forth.

He groaned against my neck. "Did you just say that you wanted to suck my cock?"

"Yes."

He let out a ragged breath. "That sounds so fucking good, but I need it somewhere else right now. Dry sex is over," growled, pulling away from my hand. Then he pressed the tip against my hole, rubbing around the outside. "How bad do you want it?"

"Fuck me, Trevor," I said, wiggling my sex against him. "Please."

He pulled my hips up for a better angle, and plunged into me.

I gasped, feeling every inch of him. Long and thick, he stretched me wide, and the pain… it was so good. Especially when he pulled back and did it again.

"Fuck, you're tight," he said through clenched teeth. "You're… not a virgin, are you?"

"No," I said, looking at him over my shoulder. "Don't stop. Keep going."

His eyes smoldered as he pulled back and began fucking me, this time not holding anything back. I closed my eyes and moaned with each glorious thrust, feeling his head hitting an inner part of me that made my entire G-spot vibrate.

Trevor grabbed the back of my hair, and wrapped it around his hand. He pulled my head back and squeezed my left breast. "Fuck… you… are… so… beautiful," he said, between thrusts.

Holding onto the hood of the car, I moaned as his hips slammed against my ass, causing the automobile to rock from the force. After a while, he slowed and leaned over me, his hand playing with my clit again.

"You gonna come for me, Kitten?" he whispered, his hips moving in a steady rhythm while he teased my nub.

I nodded, feeling myself getting closer and closer to the edge. Then, I was soaring over the cliff, screaming as the rippling waves of pleasure in my pelvis shook me to the core, giving me the release that I so desperately needed.

***

Raptor

Adriana clenched up as she came and it did me in. I thrust in and out of her a couple more times, and then quickly pulled out, shooting my load all over the crack of her ass, my own legs shaking from the intensity of the orgasm.

"Damn," I said hoarsely, still trying to catch my breath. I chuckled as I looked around, glad that boating season was over.

"Jesus, I needed that," she answered, still lying cheek-down on the hood of the car.

I zipped my pants back up, my desire for Adriana still on overdrive. I'd just came like a motherfucker, and yet I still wanted to be back inside.

Not tomorrow. Not later. But *now*. My dick was even twitching at the thought.

Adriana shivered.

"Shit, sorry. Are you cold?" I asked, rubbing the side of her thigh. She had her jacket on, but it was pulled up to her waist and her legs had goose-bumps.

She raised her head up. "I wasn't before, but I'm getting there."

I pushed her hair away from her face. Damn, she was beautiful and sex had never felt like this. Ever. Not even with Brandy. I didn't know why, since we barely knew each other, but the effect that she had on me was almost… dangerous. It made me take chances that I shouldn't have. Like having unprotected sex. I didn't even know if she was clean or not.

"Let me get something to clean you off," I said, backing away from her.

She looked at me over her shoulder. "Check the backseat. I think there's a box of tissues."

"Okay," I said, still trying to dissect what the hell was happening to me. I thought about earlier and how I'd wanted to kill the guy she'd been dancing with. The rage and jealousy that had been coursing through my veins had almost driven me over the edge. This was for a girl that I'd promised to stay away from. Meant to stay away from. After being inside of her, I knew I'd never be able to make that same promise with a straight face.

"Here," I said, cleaning off her back. "I probably should have worn a rubber."

"Probably," she said, pushing her dress back down over her hips. She turned around and raised her hands to her chest.

"Let me help you," I said, reaching for the buttons on her dress. "I suppose you're pissed off now."

She smiled up at me. "Do I look pissed?"

"You look beautiful."

"You look pretty amazing yourself," she said, running her fingers through my hair. "I think next time, however, I'm pulling *your* hair."

"Oh yeah?"

With a sparkle in her eye, she tugged on it, poking the animal inside of me. The one who liked it rough sometimes. Growling in the back of my throat, I leaned forward and kissed her lips. Hard.

Adriana pulled back, smiling. "My goodness, slow down, Raptor," she said in a breathless voice.

"Can't help it," I said, grabbing the back of her head. My zipper was already getting tight again. "You bring it out in me." I pulled her face to me and kissed her again, this time with more tenderness. But it was hard. I was already raring to go and she tasted sweet. Like peaches. I wanted to devour her lips and every other part of her.

She put her hand on my chest, gently pushing me back. "We need to leave."

Sighing, I touched her forehead with mine. "Come home with me," I whispered.

"I can't."

"Why? Because of your mother?"

"Yes. I have her car."

"What if you didn't have it? Would you?"

"I... I don't know."

"Listen to me," I said, touching the side of her face. "I know you're frightened of being with me, but I swear to you... I'll never let anything happen to you."

"You can't promise something you really have no control over," she said, looking frustrated. "We both know that."

"Bullshit. I do have control over it."

She sighed. "Like Tank had control over what happened to Krystal?"

"What happened to Krystal... that was fucked up. It was horrible. We had no idea Mud would retaliate like that. But, things are different now," I replied. "We've run The Devil's Rangers out of Iowa."

"How in the world could you do that? All of them?"

"Yup. We had proof that Mud killed Krystal and used it to drive him out. We gave him an option – move his entire Chapter to a different state, or spend the next twenty years in prison."

"You had proof? Why wouldn't you turn it over to the police? Mud needs to go to prison!"

"We take care of these kinds of things, *our* way."

"So, you just drove the club away? That's how he's going to pay for killing my best friend?"

"Believe me, when things settle, Mud's going to really pay for what he did to her. He's not going to get away with it. Tank and Slammer are already working on the details."

"See, this is exactly why I can't be around you, Trevor. You and your friends don't play by the rules."

"Yeah we do. Our rules."

"Even though they're against the law?"

"The law isn't always right."

She sighed. "It's not worth arguing with you. You're stubborn and already set in your ways."

"Exactly. So don't argue with me," I said with a cocky smile. "Just accept that things are how they are and don't worry your pretty little head about Mud and the Devil's Rangers."

"Unbelievable." She shook her head and walked to the passenger door. "Let's get out of here."

"Back to my house."

"No. To your bike. I need to get home," she said, opening the door. "And I'm pretty sure that you fucked me sober."

I got into the car. "You think you can drive?"

"I'm positive," said Adriana.

I stared at her hard. She looked sober, but I wasn't taking any chances. "Fuck that." I started the engine. "Your mother would kill me if anything ever happened to you. I'm taking you home and I'll call Tank. He can give me a ride back to my bike."

"I'm surprised that you care what my mother thinks."

"So am I," I said, rolling up the windows. "So am I."

Chapter Thirty-Seven

Adriana

Trevor drove me home and I invited him in.

"So where is your mother?" he asked as we walked into the doorway.

I flipped on the lights and looked at the clock. It was almost nine o'clock. "She should be closing the shop soon."

"I'd better get out of here then. She'll have a fucking conniption if she sees me. I don't want to be the cause of a woman having a heart-attack."

"Actually, she won't be home for another hour. They were going to grab a bite to eat before Jim dropped her off."

Trevor smiled wickedly. "We have an hour?" he said, walking toward me. "Excellent."

I put my hand on his chest. "Wait a second…"

He grabbed my hand and pulled it down to the bulge in his pants. "I only need a few," he said, kissing my neck. "Come on, Kitten. I need to be inside you again."

"I don't know," I whispered, feeling myself already responding.

Trevor pushed my jacket over my shoulders and it dropped to the floor. He picked me up and I automatically wrapped my legs around his waist. "You don't know? I think you do," he said, walking toward the steps, his hands gripping my ass tightly. "So, just let it happen."

And it did happen.

First in the bathtub, where he cleaned every part of me, using the showerhead and his tongue.

Then in my bedroom, where I finally got to see how much of his cock I could fit into my mouth.

"Stop," he said, after a few minutes.

I pulled my lips away from his penis. "What, don't you like getting a blow job?" I asked, rubbing up and down the base.

"Fuck, I love getting a blow job," he said, cupping my mound. "But I love being inside of you more."

I climbed over him and rode his cock, rocking back and forth as he held my hips, urging me faster.

"Fuck, you're so sexy," he said cupping and squeezing my breasts as I stared down at him through my hair.

Seconds later, I threw my head back, gasping as I came for a third time, this one more intense than the one I'd just had in the shower.

"Damn," he growled, flipping me onto my back and then entering me again. "I felt that, too. My turn."

I stared up at Trevor as he took charge, pounding into me. At one point, he leaned down, kissing me with a passion that I felt all the way to my toes. It made me my heart flutter, almost bringing me to tears and was enough to make me realize that I'd already fallen for him. Hard. I knew right then that I didn't want to be anywhere else but with Trevor and in his arms. Screw my mother. Screw the Gold Vipers. Screw everything else. Trevor and I were all that mattered.

He slowed down. "You okay?" he asked, touching my face.

"Only if you keep fucking me," I said, pulling his mouth back to mine so he wouldn't see the tears in my eyes.

When it was his turn to come, I could feel Trevor's cock pulsating inside of me as he stiffened up and let go, holding my hips so tightly that his fingernails dug into my skin. Then, he collapsed on top of me, both of us panting, sweaty, and spent.

"I think we should take another shower," he whispered, touching my damp forehead.

"I can but you can't. My mom's going to be home any minute."

He sighed. "Have you ever thought of moving into your own place?"

"I can't afford to. I'm in college, remember?"

He stared at me for a few seconds and then said, "Move in with me."

My eyes widened. I laughed. "Right."

He ran a finger over my arm, giving me goose-bumps. "I'm serious."

"You know, I –"

He put a finger to my lips. "Stop. Don't say anything. I just wanted to throw that out there. I know you're probably not ready for it. Hell, you're not even ready for me, are you?"

I swallowed. "Actually," I whispered. "I've been doing some thinking."

"Thinking?" He grinned. "Sounds like trouble."

I slugged him in the arm.

"Just giving you shit, darlin'. Now, tell me, what exactly were you thinking?"

"We should keep seeing each other. But maybe keep it on the down low right now."

He smirked. "The down low, huh?"

"Yeah."

"What you mean is keep it from your mother?"

I nodded.

He sighed. "Kitten, you shouldn't be lying to her."

"Yeah, but…"

"But, nothing. She's your mother and you're an adult. Tell her the truth."

"The truth," I repeated, now smirking myself.

"Yes," he said, grabbing both my hands. He turned them over and kissed my knuckles. "Tell her you've fallen for me and there's nothing she can do about it."

He already knew it, too. I had definitely fallen for him.

"And then I will tell her that she needs to trust me. That I'll never let anything happen to her daughter."

"Easier said than done," I said. "You've met her. You know she doesn't listen to you."

"That's her problem then."

I sighed.

"What do you want from me?" he asked, his eyes burning into mine. "I mean, really?"

"The same thing you want from me," I said, not really sure exactly what I was ready for. I could pretty much guess what he wanted, however. Sex. Lots of it.

"And what is that?"

"This," I said.

"You mean, sex?"

I nodded.

He smiled in amusement. "Is that it? You just want me to fuck you?"

"Isn't that what you want?"

His face became serious. "Honestly? I want much more than that. I want you on the back of my bike. I want you sitting next to me in the morning, while we're eating breakfast. I want you picking out sheets for our bed. I want to know what your favorite kind of pizza is or how you like your burgers. I want to know what kind of perfume you wear, because it drives me insane. Do I want *sex*? Fuck yes. But I also want everything else, Kitten. That's what I want from you."

I couldn't help it. I smiled, my stomach full of butterflies as I imagined waking up to him every morning and eating breakfast. Taking showers together. Shopping at Home Depot. Decorating our Christmas tree together. It all sounded so romantic.

He smiled back. "You have no idea how beautiful you are when you smile. No idea."

I was about to tell him that he wasn't so bad on the eyes when I heard the front door open.

"Fuck, my mother," I said, jumping out of his arms.

He growled.

"Okay, um... just, stay here until she goes to bed. I'll drive you back to your bike afterward," I said, pulling my robe on.

"Fine," he said, looking pissed.

"You're mad at me," I said, watching him get out of bed.

"I'm frustrated," he said, walking toward my bathroom where his clothes were spread out on the floor.

Sighing, I slipped out of my bedroom and met my mother by the stairs.

"Hi, honey. How was the reception?" she asked, yawning.

"It was... very sad."

"I'm sure. I called Bonnie and left her a message. The poor woman," she said with a somber expression. "I just can't imagine what today was like. Seeing your daughter buried like that."

"I know," I said, suddenly feeling guilty about the last couple of hours. My best friend was in the ground and I'd been acting like a sex addict who'd finally gotten her fix.

Although, Krystal probably would have been proud...

A loud thud from inside of my bedroom startled us both.

"What's that noise?" she asked, pushing past me to my door.

Fuck!

I followed her in, ready for an argument.

"Keep this window closed," she said, moving to my bedroom window. "It's cold outside. You'll get sick."

I looked around, shocked that Trevor wasn't inside. Then I realized that he'd climbed out the window, which I'd done quite a few times myself as a teenager. He was quite a bit heavier than me, however, and it made me wonder if the trellis was broken.

Mom closed the window and locked it. Then she turned to smile at me. "Guess what?"

"What?" I asked, moving next to her. I looked outside, but didn't see any sign of him.

"Jim asked me if I wanted to go away with him for a weekend in January."

I turned around, surprised. "Are you?"

"I think so," she said, her cheeks flushed. "He owns a cabin up north, and wants to take me snowmobiling and ice-fishing."

"You should go. It will be good for you."

"I'm definitely going to consider it," she replied, walking toward the door. "He's such a nice man. So thoughtful and polite."

"He seems very nice from what I can tell."

Her eyes sparkled. "You know, he has a nephew who's single. A dentist."

I groaned. "Don't even think about trying to set me up."

"Maybe we'll invite him over for Thanksgiving."

"Mom…"

She grinned. "You should give him a chance, Adriana."

"Like you gave Trevor?"

Her smile vanished. "That was different, and you know it."

"Trevor's a nice guy, Mom. He really is."

"I don't care how nice he is," she replied. "He hangs out with bad people. You and I both know it. Look at what happened to Krystal."

"That wasn't Trevor's fault."

She sighed wearily. "Are you really going to rehash all of this? I thought you were through with him anyway."

"Maybe I am. Maybe I'm not."

Her lips pursed. "I knew when I saw him at the funeral there would be trouble. I just knew it."

I rubbed my forehead. "There wasn't any trouble."

"Right. That's why you're bringing him up?"

"Seriously, Mom, I'm tired of you treating me like a child," I said, resisting the urge to stomp my foot.

"Then start thinking and acting like a level-headed adult."

"You know, I think I know what my problem is," I said, more to myself.

"That you're too trustworthy with men?" she replied. "Or that you think you can change them? Because you can't. Especially someone like him. Someone who doesn't want to change."

I glared at her. "No. My problem is that I let *you* run my life."

Her eyes widened. "That's not fair."

"Not fair? Mom, I'm twenty-one years old. You insist on doing my laundry, cooking my meals, even picking out my makeup. You've not only spoiled the hell out of me, but you've made me feel like I owe you."

"What do you mean, I make you feel like you owe me?"

"I just…" I stammered. "I just feel like I'm living your life and not my own sometimes. You wanted me to work at the shop, so I did. You're the one who talked me into my college classes, you're the one who picked out my car. You even make my salon appointments when you think I need a haircut. It's just so frustrating."

"Well, I'm sorry," she said, her eyes filling with tears. "You're my daughter and all I have left. Maybe I coddle you a little too much, but that's what mothers do. I just want what's best for you."

"Mom, you're not just coddling me, you're smothering me."

"You're exaggerating."

"Am I? Hell, maybe Trevor is bad for me or maybe he's the best thing that ever happened. But, I won't know the truth if I continue letting you make all my decisions. You have to stop and I have to quit allowing it to happen."

She raised her hands in the air. "Fine, you want to risk your life by hanging out with a hoodlum like Trevor? Do it, but don't come crying to me when he breaks your heart, or ends up in jail."

"Mom, you have to try and trust my judgment a little better," I said, softening my voice. "I'm not out to risk my life. I'm not going to be joining their club. I just want to get to know Trevor better, and if I find out that he's really no good for me, at least it's my decision not to see him. Not yours."

She wiped a couple tears from under her eyes. "If anything ever happened to you, I don't know what I'd do," she said. "Please, if you're going to see him, be careful, Adriana."

I took her hands in mine. "Mom, I swear to you, I'll jump ship the moment anything gets dangerous or weird. Okay? I promise."

"You'd better."

I sighed and gave her a hug.

"Don't you really want to work at the shop?" she asked.

I pulled away. "I don't know. I mean, I guess it's fine for now and I do appreciate that you're letting me work there. But, once I graduate from college, I'll probably move on."

"I understand that. But, remember, when I die, the company is going to be yours. You need to know how to run it. It's our legacy, Adriana."

I groaned. "Fine, but quit talking about dying. That shouldn't happen for a very long time, Mom."

"One can only hope, but we both know that you can't predict the future," she said.

"But, we choose the path that leads us to it," I finished for her. "Yes, I know."

She sighed wearily. "Well, I'm going to take a shower and then make some tea. Would you like a cup? It's decaffeinated."

"No. I'm going to take a shower and get ready for bed, too. But, thank you."

"I love you, Adriana. I've only always wanted what's best for you. You know that, right?"

"I know and I love you, too, Mom. More than anything."

She smiled sadly and left my room.

Chapter Thirty-Eight

RAPTOR

After I almost broke my fucking neck climbing out of Adriana's window, I called Tank.

"Can you pick me up, brother?" I asked, walking away from her place. As I passed by several houses, I could see people watching me through their curtains. Snooping.

Old Geezers.

"Where the fuck you at?" he asked. I could hear music in the background and a girl giggling.

"Just left Adriana's place. I need a ride to my bike."

"Where is it?"

I told him.

He sighed. "Yeah, give me an address and I'll shoot over there in twenty minutes."

"Why twenty?"

"Because I was in the middle of almost getting my dick waxed when you called," he snapped.

"Then you probably only need three minutes," I joked.

He chuckled. "You ain't kidding. This chick is double-jointed, man. She can twist her body and munch her own box if she wanted to."

I laughed. Apparently he was now dealing with Krystal's death much better than he was earlier. "Where'd you meet her?"

"She's friends with one of the strippers. I should take a picture of her and send it to you. Doll, can you wrap your ankles over your neck again?"

"No pictures. Just, hurry up. I need to get my bike."

"Fine. I'll see if I can get her to give me a quick blow, since I've got to come and pick your ass up."

"Sorry."

"Bros before Hoes," he whispered and then let out a ragged breath. "Double jointed, though, man. You owe me."

"Get her number."

"Fucking right I will."

I noticed there was a coffee shop up the street. I told him about it.

"Yeah, I think I know where that is."

"It's closed but I'll be waiting for you on the bench outside. Call me if you get lost."

"I doubt anyone can get lost in Jensen," he replied.

After we hung up, I sent Adriana a text, letting her know where I was. She called me back.

"Guess what?' she said, a smile in her voice.

"What?"

"I told my mother about us."

I grunted. "Really. How'd she take it?"

"She's not exactly thrilled, but… she's not going to interfere."

"Good. I didn't like sneaking out of your bedroom like that. Not only did I bend your trellis, but I felt like a punk ass kid slipping away in the night."

"You bent the trellis?"

"Yeah, I can fix it though. No worries."

"Where are you?"

"I'm heading toward that coffee shop, Bella's Brews. Tank is picking me up."

"That's nice of him."

"He's a real sweetheart, all right," I said, grinning. "We're BFFs you know."

She giggled."

"What are you doing tomorrow?"

"I have classes."

"What about after?"

"To be honest, I'm usually really busy during the week with homework and school."

"What about dinner? Or lunch? You have time for that?"

She was silent for a couple seconds. "I'll make time."

"Good. I'll pick you up and bring you back to my place when you're free."

"To eat?"

"Oh, I'll be eating pie. You can do whatever you want," I said, imaging her riding my face again.

She breathed in sharply. "You're so bad."

"You like it when I'm bad. Admit it."

She giggled. "I'll call you tomorrow. Between classes. Okay?"

"I'm counting on it."

"Goodnight."

"Goodnight, Kitten."

Chapter Thirty-Nine

RAPTOR

Tank picked me up in his dad's black Suburban.

"So, how was the reception?" he asked, as we drove back toward it.

"Good."

"You work things out with Adriana?"

I grinned. "Yes I did. A few times."

He chuckled. "Can I smell your finger? I didn't get any tonight. Least you can let me do."

I held up my middle finger.

Tank laughed.

"Didn't you get your BJ?"

His smile fell. "No. She took off. I'm supposed to call her tomorrow."

"You going to?"

"She's a fucking contortionist. Of course I'm going to call her."

I laughed.

"So, you going to make Adriana your Old Lady now, or what?"

"As far as I'm concerned, she is my Old Lady."

"You need to make it official."

"I will. Just need to ease her into it."

"Ease her into it? You must really dig this chick," he said, pulling out a pack of cigarettes. "You mind?"

I was probably one of the only guys in the club that didn't smoke. "No," I said, cracking a window.

"Fuck, I still can't believe those fuckheads killed her, man," he said, lighting his cigarette.

"What's the deal on that? We coming down hard on them, or what?"

"Hell, yeah. We have to be careful though. The Old Man still isn't sure who the informant is."

"I have no fucking clue either."

He was silent for a few minutes. "So, this is how it's going to be – we're going to lay low for a couple of months, and then when the time comes, blow their fucking club up. Take everyone in that Chapter out. That way the word on the streets will be that nobody fucks with us or our women. Nobody."

Taking them all out seemed extreme to me, but I wasn't the one making those decisions. "You know where they set up their new camp?"

"Yeah. They're north. Up in Minnesota. Hayward, I think. It's only four hours away."

"Huh."

He grinned darkly. "It's going to be beautiful, brother. Beautiful. I'm going to take Mud out myself."

"The Mother Chapter is going to want to retaliate," I said, knowing that the rest of the Devil's Rangers wouldn't stand for it.

"We'll worry about that when the time comes," he said. "Besides, Pop says he's already talked to Bastard."

Bastard was the original founder of the Gold Vipers. An old vet who still led the Mother Chapter in Sacramento.

"What he say?"

"We wouldn't be going forward if he wasn't backing us."

"Shit's going to get ugly."

"Far as I'm concerned, it can't get any uglier than it already is," said Tank, clenching his teeth. "Not after what they did to Krystal."

I held out my fist.

He smacked it with his.

Chapter Forty

Adriana

For the next three weeks, Trevor and I spent as much time together as we could. When we weren't making love, we were taking walks, renting movies, or he was teaching me how to cook.

"I have to say, this is a good fucking omelet," he said one morning after I'd stayed overnight. I'd made him something called a "Denver Omelet." I'd found the recipe online. "Your cooking skills have greatly improved."

"I have a good teacher," I said, smiling as I poured him another glass of orange juice. His compliment made me giddy, though. I actually enjoyed cooking and wanted to please him. It was a trait I knew had come from my mother. Making her man happy.

He set his fork down on his empty plate and pulled me onto his lap. "This is great, isn't it?" he whispered, moving my hair to the side. "I mean, it feels like were married sometimes. I like it."

I grinned. "You do?"

He kissed my lips. "Don't you?"

"I guess so. I mean, I know sometimes married couples don't have sex very often," I teased.

"That's never going to be us," he said. "In fact," he gulped down his orange juice and then pushed everything off of the kitchen table and onto the linoleum, startling the hell out of me.

"Trevor!"

"Don't worry. I'll take care of it."

"Good." Although nothing broke, there was still a mess.

"What are you doing?" I asked as he stood up and walked over to the refrigerator. He grabbed a bottle of maple syrup and walked back over.

"I need dessert," he said, grabbing the front of the white muscle shirt I was wearing. The one he'd loaned me.

"Dessert?"

He ripped the cotton away from my chest and tossed it aside. With one hand on my right breast, he reached down for my panties.

"Don't you dare rip them; they're my best pair."

Trevor grabbed me around the waist, picked me up, and set me down on the table. Then he pulled my underwear down and placed them by his nose. "Mm… they smell nice, too."

My face turned red.

Chuckling, he pushed me down on the table and wrapped my legs over his shoulders. His face became serious. "I'm going to make you come so hard, darlin'." There was a hungry fierceness in his eyes that made me instantly wet. "Then I'm going to fuck the shit out of you until you're screaming my name and I'm coming all over your beautiful body. Afterward, we're going to go and buy you some new panties. The crotchless kind, so I can *take* you anywhere and everywhere. You feel me?"

My throat became so dry that I had to swallow. "Yes. I feel you, Trevor."

He grabbed the bottle of syrup and held it over my crotch. My eyes widened as I realized what he was about to do.

"Are you really —" I asked as he squeezed the bottle. I squealed as the cold syrup hit my labia and dribbled down. I shivered. "It's… cold."

He set the bottle down and grabbed my hips. "This is where I warm it up."

When Trevor's lips touched my sex and he began licking, I gasped in delight.

"Mm… that's yummy," he whispered, flicking his tongue up, down, and around my clit.

Moaning, I grabbed his head, wrapping my fingers in his hair as he sucked and devoured the maple syrup. Then he added his fingers, pressing deep, finding that spot while his tongue worked that magic on my nub. He kept a steady rhythm as the pressure began to build and the need to release became more and more intense. Soon, I was squirming and pushing against his face, pulling at his hair, and squeezing my nipples all at the same time, until he added just enough pressure to make me scream out an orgasm that rocked me to the core.

"That's my girl," he said huskily.

"Oh, my God, Trevor," I said, trying to catch my breath.

He stood up and shoved his jeans to the floor. "I'm not finished with you," he said, pulling me off the table. Grabbing my by the hips, he turned me around and bent me over his dinette. Then he was ramming into me, his hands on my breasts, both of us grunting like wild animals.

"I love this," he growled into my ear as he leaned over me, pounding away at my pussy. "I love you. Fuck, I love you."

"I love you, too," I replied, my eyes filling with tears.

Gasping, he thrust into me two more times, and then stiffened up as he came, holding me so tightly that I could barely breathe.

"Trevor, too tight," I whispered hoarsely.

He chuckled and released me. "Sorry," he said, pulling out.

"It's okay."

He turned me around and looked into my eyes. "You are on the pill, right?"

"Yes," I replied. "I told you that last week."

"Good, but I just want you to know that if anything ever happened, I'd take care of you and the baby. You know that."

I nodded.

He relaxed. "So, did you mean it?" he asked, smiling again. "Do you really love me?"

"Yes," I said, grinning up at him. "I love you, Trevor."

He pulled a strand of my hair. "I love you, too. I wasn't just saying it."

"I didn't think you were."

"I want you to be my Old Lady," he said suddenly.

I stiffened up. I knew how much this meant to bikers. I just wasn't sure if I liked the idea of being just his 'Old Lady'. "Explain exactly what that means."

"You're my woman. Nobody else will mess with you. You're going to wear my patch, Kitten."

"So, in the biker world, you wear a patch. Not a… ring."

He grinned. "I'll get you a ring, too, babe."

"As in..."

"An engagement ring," he said. "I want you to marry me."

My eyes widened in shock. "Marriage?"

"Eventually. Isn't that what you want?"

"I…" I smiled. "Yes. Of course." I felt so much love for him in that moment that I didn't think I'd want anything less.

He kissed my knuckles. "Well, then. That's that. We patch you, first, and then once you're finished with school, we get hitched."

"Okay."

"When do you want to tell your mother?"

I sighed. She was going to flip her lid. "Do we have to? Maybe we could tell her on our fifth anniversary?"

He chuckled. "I hear you, darlin', but she needs to know. She's going to be a grandmother someday. I want kids, you know. Lots of them."

"Okay," I replied, excited that he wanted kids. Something told me he was going to be a wonderful father. "We'll tell her. *After* you get me a ring."

"She's going to know when we buy the ring," he said. "Obviously."

"Oh yeah," I said, laughing nervously.

"You know we can't go anywhere else to buy you a ring. She already dislikes me. If I went to another jeweler, she'll really fucking hate me."

"True," I said, my stomach already in a multitude of knots as I thought about telling her.

"It's going to be all right," he said, staring into my eyes. "I'll take care of you. You know that, right?"

"I know."

"Good," he said, kissing me again. "Now, why don't you go and take a shower. I'll clean up and then we'll go and talk to Slammer about our plans."

"Okay," I said.

I left the kitchen, feeling nervous about the whole thing. Although I loved him, I was still scared about what it meant. Now, I'd have to wear a patch, not to mention a ring. I'd promised my mother that I'd keep the biker world separate from what he and I had together. But now, I knew it couldn't be. It was all or nothing.

As I took my shower, I began to relax. I'd met some of his friends who were in the Gold Vipers the last couple of weeks, and they seemed nice. Their Old Ladies had also been very cool. They weren't at all what I'd pictured them to be and were definitely not pushovers. In fact, they seemed very independent and well respected.

I can do this, I thought, drying myself off with the towel. *I will do this.*

After I got dressed, I walked out of the bathroom and that's when I heard him arguing with someone.

"It's not mine," said Trevor in a firm voice.

"It is yours, Trevor. He's sterile and you're the only other person I've been with."

My heart stopped.

It was Brandy.

"You're lying," he said loudly.

She began to cry. "No, I'm not. Listen to me, we can do this. Didn't you always say that you wanted a son, Trevor? Now we can have one. We can start over."

"I don't want to start over with you, Brandy. We're done."

I turned the corner and both of them looked at me.

"She's pregnant?" I asked, my voice hollow.

"Yes, I am," she said haughtily.

He gave her a venomous look. "So she says, I doubt it's mine."

"But, it could be?" I asked.

"It's yours, Trevor! We were together six weeks ago. I'm six weeks pregnant!"

I'd known him for five.

I grabbed my purse and walked toward the stairs.

"Wait a second, where are you going?" he asked, coming up behind me.

I turned around. Deep down in my gut, I knew the baby was his. I just knew it. "Obviously you two need to work things out," I said, my eyes filling with tears.

"Bullshit," he said. "She can leave. Not you."

"Trevor, I'm carrying your child. We've known each other for two years. You're going to kick me out of here for *her*?" snapped Brandy.

He turned around and pointed his finger at her. "Shut the fuck up, Brandy. You can't just walk back into my life, say you're pregnant, and think that everything is going to go the way you want it. Even if it's my fucking kid."

I let out a ragged sigh and headed downstairs for the door.

He flew down them and grabbed my arm. "Wait. Don't you leave me, Adriana."

"Could this baby be yours?'

He sighed loudly. "I don't know. There's a chance, I guess. It happened before I met you. It was a mistake, obviously." He pulled me into his arms. "I hope to fuck that you believe it."

I nodded.

"I'll make her leave," he whispered into my hair.

I pulled away. "No. I'll leave. You two have a lot to talk about."

He rubbed the back of his neck and laughed angrily. "This is such fucking bullshit."

"I know. Call me."

Trevor's face was filled with anguish as he pulled me into his arms and kissed me deeply. "I love you," he said, releasing me.

"I love you, too," I answered, turning away quickly to avoid his eyes.

"I'll call you."

All I could do was nod, I was so choked up.

After I left the house, I cried.

Now that she was pregnant, I knew our relationship was doomed. I was so upset, that I stopped and grabbed a bag of fast-food, not even sure what I'd ordered. I brought it back home and scarfed it all down. Ten minutes later, I threw it all up and cried some more.

***

Trevor didn't call me until the next day. He apologized and said that Brandy was going to go in for DNA testing in the next couple of months, to make sure the baby was really his.

"So, where is she now?" I asked.

He was quiet.

"Did she leave?"

He sighed. "I let her move in."

My heart stopped. "What?"

"She doesn't have anywhere to go, but listen to me. I hate that fucking bitch. She's only here because if she *is* carrying my child, I want to protect him."

He was already calling the baby, 'him'.

"I understand," I said, the tears spilling from my eyes. He wasn't breaking up with me but it sure felt the same. My heart was being crushed and neither of us were really even responsible.

"Are you crying?"

"No," I lied.

"I love you, Adriana. No matter what happens, I still want to marry you. Even if this baby is mine, this thing won't affect 'us'. You feel me?"

"Yes," I lied again. Somehow I knew that if the baby was his, it was over for us. Really over.

Turns out that we were both wrong. Things definitely changed and Brandy wasn't the only one... pregnant.

***

End Of Book One

Available May 2015

Printed in Great Britain
by Amazon.co.uk, Ltd.,
Marston Gate.